HOUSE DIVIDED

A POLITICAL SATIRE

D0885610

Also by Bruce Campbell

If Chins Could Kill: Confessions of a B Movie Actor
Make Love the Bruce Campbell Way
Hail to the Chin: Further Confessions of a B Movie Actor
The Cool Side of My Pillow: A Book of Essays

HOUSE DIVIDED

A POLITICAL SATIRE

by

BRUCE CAMPBELL

EASTMOOR MEDIA™

Copyright © 2021 by Bruce Campbell.

All rights reserved. No part of this book may be reproduced in any form without written permission from the copyright owner, except for the use of quotations in a book review.

Eastmoor Media logo is a trademark of Campbell Entertainment, Inc.

ISBN 978-1-7368511-1-1

I

THE PLACE

Oregon, particularly in the rural areas, has always been an interesting, mixed bag of humanity. A single, small valley could contain a hippie commune, an ex-Ford executive, a jihadist training camp, or wealthy refugees, fleeing the craziness of San Francisco. Oregonians love religion, guns, opiates, no sales tax, dogs, beer, pick-up trucks and pot.

People born in Oregon work hard and play hard. They tend to like who they are and will defend their right to do whatever they damn well please by any means necessary. Oregonians are not lovers of Big Government. They don't like being told what to do or be bossed around.

Enough rural folks are pissed off that they want to form their own, breakaway state.

People who move to Oregon are often in the process of re-inventing their lives. It's a great state to move to after a divorce, or a mid-life crisis, or when you finally decide to clean up your act and are ready for a big change – including your name. Oregon is where a Debbie can become "Radiance," and a Larry can now be called "River" – all with a straight face.

Politically, Oregon runs the full spectrum, from Proud Boys on the right to Antifa on the left. The sides are so far apart, the fact that anything gets done in the state is a marvel.

Dryer County lies in eastern Oregon and relies on ranching, logging and a federal prison for its revenue. Election season has rolled around and it's usually uneventful, since the same county officials get re-elected over and over.

But this season has shaped up to be . . . *different.*

II

THE CANDIDATES

It's not hard to get "rural" in Dryer County. 85% of the county boasts a population of less than two people per square mile – the yardstick which used to measure when they closed "the Frontier" at the turn of the last century.

One such rural retreat, five miles from town, was an old, large farmhouse, which had become "Hippie Chic" over the years. Prayer flags draped from mature oak trees and the rickety, now-grey picket fence surrounding the house.

Getting ready for an event in his bedroom, Alan Rosenbaum – a full-blown hippie in his forties

— rummaged through an overstuffed hemp bag and produced a couple of colorful scarves, adjusting them carefully around his neck.

~

Back in Dryer, a new development, "Palm Harbor," with neither a "palm" nor a "harbor" in evidence, offered three different floor plans.

One such home — with the "Sunset" floorplan — flew an enormous American flag from its front porch, which was reflected in the side of an enormous Hummer parked out front.

In the master bedroom, getting ready for the same event, was Sean Heston, a "squaresville" man in his fifties. Ramrod straight, with a military bearing, he reached for a red, white and blue tie — among similar ones in his closet — and tied a tight Windsor.

As the two men prepared, their differences also revealed their similarities:

Alan sorted through a basket of bracelets and slipped a few on his wrist. Sean picked his US-made Detroit Watch Company watch with the black band and tightened it.

Alan poured some patchouli out of a crude glass container and spread it ceremoniously around his neck and chest. Sean popped the lid on his Old Spice aftershave and gave himself a few squirts.

Alan tied a leather headband, decorated with small gems, around his mass of hair, containing it. Sean ran a comb through his salt and pepper hair, meticulously creating a razor-straight part.

Alan fired up a doobie and huffed it a couple times. Sean unscrewed the lid of his well-worn flask and took a shot of liquid courage. He exhaled hotly. Alan exhaled deeply also, blowing the skunky-smelling smoke into the air.

From another room, an older woman's voice remarked, "I keep wondering whether I raised an idiot or a moron."

Alan walked into the family living room to face his mother, Esther. The whole place had a worn, over-the-hill hippie feel. Esther was also a hippie – and a formidable personality.

"Why would you say that?" Alan asked.

"You're a liberal Jew from the Midwest running for office against a local Christian conservative – in a conservative county in rural Oregon," Esther replied. "Idiot? Moron? You decide."

"Mother, there are progressive people everywhere – even out here. I'm just going to offer a rational alternative. I will appeal to the peaceful side of these Christians."

"Bullshit. You need to crucify him."

"Mom, please!" Alan pleaded.

~ ·

Sean stepped into his tract home living room and was met by Doris, his picture-perfect, impossibly blonde wife. "Looking sharp, sir," she said.

Sean kissed Doris on the lips. "You ain't looking so bad yourself, rock of my life," then, loudly, "Inspection!"

Sean's son Ronald (named after the president) ran into the room and stood at attention. He was dressed exactly like his father. Same hair style too.

Sean approached, like a drill sergeant, for the once over. "Let's have a look. This is our first debate. It's going to be televised."

"On *local cable* . . ." Ronald replied, unimpressed.

"That's why we have to look our best," Sean said, before looking at Ronald's shoes. "You're going to want to get that scuff off."

"Yes, sir. How long will this last?" he asked.

"Just an hour, honey. You can do it," Doris replied.

"An hour! I'll die!"

"That's enough of that," Sean said, inspecting Ronald's part. "We are the Heston family. We are proud Americans. Your father has chosen to serve his community and we need to show our unified, unwavering support."

Sean grabbed a comb out of his pocket and handed it to Ronald. "Have another go at that. It's gotta be one thin line. You're all over the place."

"Yes, sir . . ." and he was off.

Sean turned to Doris. "Speaking of unwavering support, where is Nancy? Is she ready? Is she even awake?"

Doris gestured down the hall. "In her room."

Sean started for her room, but Doris stopped him. "Sean . . . you know I don't usually get involved in your affairs, so I only have one piece of advice for the debate tonight," she offered. "TV is media and media is social media and social media is forever. You say something you regret these days, you can't take it back."

"I appreciate that, honey," Sean said, a little prickly. "But in politics, authenticity gets elected. I can't be who I'm not."

"No, dear. Of course not," Doris assured, before straightening his tie. "It's just that sometimes, your assertiveness comes across as . . . a-hole-ness."

Sean looked to the ceiling and exhaled. "Ok. I'll try not to be an . . . a-hole."

Doris pecked Sean on his cheek and headed out. Sean looked to the closed bedroom door of his daughter.

~

Alan stuffed a bunch of loose papers into his hemp satchel.

"You know Sean Heston's wife is shtupping her Pilates instructor," Esther said.

Alan looked up in horror. "What? How do you know that?"

"It's common knowledge among the hair salon set," Esther explained. "And Mr. Incumbent is not about to ascend any time soon either, I can tell you. That man would hump a rock!"

"Mother. Stop filling my head full of negative imagery!"

"You need to expose his hypocrisy. He's so fucking sanctimonious, I wanna barf!"

"I will expose his lack of sensitivity for the poor and downtrodden in Dryer County," Alan said, as calmy as he could muster.

"You're doomed."

Alan gathered up his car keys, bound in a leather token. "Even if I lose, I win, mom. More exposure for what I'm promoting is still good for my business."

"Your 'self-help' business. Listen, buster, if you can't help yourself, who can you?" Esther asked pointedly.

"My work is a journey for both healer and client, mother."

"Spare me the new age bullshit. If you don't kick this prick in the balls – and hard – he will roll over you . . . like your father."

Alan bolted for the door. "Not necessary, Mom."

"SO necessary, Alan."

Slam! Alan was gone.

~

KNOCK-KNOCK.

"Nancy? You ready?" Sean asked, outside Nancy's door. "Big day today. I'm sure you're excited."

No answer.

Then, Sean wrinkled his nose, smelling something disagreeable. "Nancy. Is that marijuana I smell? You open this door right now!"

"It's not locked," Nancy said, from behind the door.

Surprised, Sean let himself in.

Nancy Heston, Sean's goth-wannabe teenage daughter, was coming back in from the balcony as Sean entered. She was dressed in uncomfortable, formal clothing. "Yes dad, you smell marijuana."

"What the hell, Nancy!" Sean exclaimed. "I can't get re-elected with a pothead for a kid!"

"If it's all about you, yeah, I could see how that would be a problem."

"It's illegal, for starters."

"Not in this state. Fully recreational," Nancy reminded him.

"You're not 21! And it's not legal federally."

"It should be."

"That shit rots your developing brain," Sean said, jabbing a finger.

"So does bourbon, dad," Nancy countered. "Or in mom's case, Xanax and Chablis. Maybe I should smoke cigarettes like you!"

"Don't get lippy with me, young lady."

"Deny it, Marlboro Man. Marlboro Light, anyway."

Sean hesitated. Busted.

"I have a nose too, dad," Nancy said.

Sean waved his hands in the air. "Okay, enough of this conversation. I have a debate to win and I expect you to attend, STONED or not!"

"Fine. Now that I'm stoned, I can handle this freak show."

Sean headed for the door and bellowed to the entire house, "Wheels up in five minutes!"

~

At Esther's overgrown hippie haven, faded prayer flags twirled in the late afternoon breeze. Alan opened the door of his mid-nineties Prius. His low budget, magnetized campaign sign was stuck on the side of the car:

Rosenbaum
Help Me
Help You
Help Us

~

Sean strutted out of his chronically tidy home, followed by his dutiful family. Everything was ship shape, particularly his imposing Humvee, which gleamed in the driveway – an American flag decal was "wrapped," Hollywood-style, around the entire vehicle.

As Sean's family climbed in the enormous vehicle, his campaign slogan emblazoned on the side was visible for all to see:

Commissioner
Sean Heston
Suck It Up America!

III

THE EVENT

Alan drove along, oblivious. Suddenly, through an open window, a measly fly buzzed in and landed on his dashboard. "Oh. Hello, little fly. Did you get lost? Don't worry. I'll help you to freedom."

Alan reached for the fly, but it took off, buzzing about the inside of his car. Concentrating on the fly, Alan forgot about steering.

In the bike lane, a cyclist in spandex was cruising along the side of the road. Alan's Prius, no longer being piloted, veered into the guy, forcing his bike into a row of mailboxes.

Alan was clueless to the impact. He was laser-focused on the fly, but no closer to catching it. "You are clever and agile! Such a symbol of the diversity of life!"

Meanwhile, Sean was driving with purpose in his muscular Humvee, his brochure-ready family seated obediently. Nancy was in attendance, but would rather be anywhere else.

Ahead of them, the same cyclist, banged up from his wreck with the Prius, wobbled down the road.

The Humvee approached from behind and crowded the cyclist aggressively, not passing, just revving its engine and honking.

Doris looked at Sean like he was crazy. "Honey, just go past. He's in the new bike lane."

"I didn't vote for it," Sean said, as he laid on the horn.

The weary cyclist had had enough and he flipped off the Humvee.

Sean gripped the wheel in a fury. "Kale sucking commie!"

Screeech! The massive Humvee swerved directly into the shocked cyclist and knocked his bike through another row of mailboxes.

Self-satisfied, Sean glanced in the rear-view mirror at the carnage left in his wake. His family was mortified.

"Jesus, dad, you might have killed that guy!" Nancy exclaimed.

"One less liberal in the world. You're welcome, America!"

~

The Dryer Elks Lodge was a relic of days gone by. Outdated cars parked outside while a geriatric crowd of locals shuffled in.

Sean's Humvee arrived with a CRASH as it wiped out a decorative planter on the sidewalk. Sean stepped out, triumphantly waving to the slow-moving crowd.

A local news crew – of one person – approached Sean. Cindy Chan, the local reporter for KDRY-TV, held out her microphone. "Mr. Heston, are you ready for tonight's debate?"

Sean chuckled. "Are you kidding, Cindy? I grew up as a scrappy ranch hand in the Owyhee backcountry. I'm ready for anything."

With a quick nod, Sean plowed toward the entrance, his family a block behind.

Alan's car finally rolled into the parking lot. He opened his dusty door, cupping something in his hands. "Here you go, little Frodo the fly. Fly. Fly free, like the dove of peace!"

Alan released the beleaguered fly into the desert air, said a little prayer and clapped two times.

At the entrance, Cindy approached Alan. "Mr. Rosencrans. . ."

"*Rosenbaum,*" Alan corrected.

"Uh, of course. Sir, as the clear underdog in this race for county commissioner, what would you say makes you most qualified to serve?"

Alan smiled at the question. "I just saved a fly . . ."

Cindy stared blankly as Alan clicked twice and slipped inside.

~

Locals milled about the ancient hall excitedly, drinking coffee and catching up. The Mayor, Dobb Dryer, stepped up on the decorative platform and fiddled with his microphone, blowing into it a few times. "Now, folks, we're about ready here, so please take your seats."

As people settled in, Sean and Alan made their way up to the stage – Sean to a seat on the right and Alan to a seat on the left. Two Scouts, Oscar Vasquez and Madison Jenkins, took seats between them.

"I'm Mayor Dobb Dryer. Most of you know me, I guess . . ."

A ripple of familiar laughter spread across the crowd.

Dobb smiled. "The Dryer Elks is proud to host this evening's debate, which is sponsored by our local Scout chapter 944. We have a couple of future Eagle Scouts here, who will walk us through the ground rules. Please welcome Oscar Vasquez and Madison Jenkins."

Polite applause as the Scouts stepped up to the podium, scripts in hand.

Madison cleared her throat and began. "Good evening, ladies and gentlemen. The topic of tonight's debate is Conflict Resolution."

Madison nodded to Oscar, who peeled open his handwritten note. "The world has many conflicts today. Some are resolved through violence. Some are resolved peace . . . peaceably . . ."

Madison continued. "Each candidate for county commissioner will share their views on the subject, then take questions from the audience."

"We urge all participants to be civil and constructive," Oscar added.

The Scouts took a seat to the same polite applause.

"All, right. Thank you, Scouts," Dobb said, addressing the crowd. "Let's get to know our candidates. Up first is a man who needs no introduction in Dryer County. This incumbent is a God-fearing, devoted husband and father of two who served his county proudly as a veteran of Operation Desert Storm. Let's watch his campaign ad . . ."

On a much-used projection screen, Sean's ad unspooled. An overly-dramatic voice narrated the ad: "Real Americans love America. Sean Heston is an American, so he loves America. Sean fought overseas for our American freedom. He loves freedom too – almost as much as he loves America – because nobody loves America like Sean Heston loves America."

The ad was full of explosions, guns, religious imagery and Sean in front of a giant American flag, saluting like general Patton. The music swelled as the announcer concluded with Sean's campaign slogan: "Suck it up, America!"

The crowd ate it up and applauded enthusiastically.

Dobb beamed. "Please welcome incumbent County Commissioner, Mr. Sean Heston!"

Sean stepped up to his podium and nodded appreciatively at the warm reception. His front row family clapped dutifully. Nancy struggled with cotton mouth.

"His challenger, somewhat new to these parts . . ." Dobb began, before having to check his notes. "Alan . . . Rose . . ."

Alan was used to this and corrected the mayor: "*Rosenbaum.*"

"Yes, of course," Dobb continued, "Mr. Rosenbaum is a self-help guru, originally from Detroit . . ."

The crowd gasped at the mention of that rough, dangerous city.

". . . He specializes in . . . Cranial . . . Sacral therapy, lives with his mother and enjoys the *Games of the Thrones.*"

There were a few nervous coughs and a general shifting in seats.

Dobb gestured to the screen. "Let's watch his campaign ad . . ."

As the obtuse images unfolded, Alan narrated his own ad: "Fossil fuels only fuel human hatred. More Fuels, more hatred. The siren sings the song of love. Guns are like glue, that stick to you. Change is the only thing that is real."

Alan's ad was incomprehensible – like Terrence Malik on Xanax. He took his sweet time speaking his slogan as reflective, cloudy images rolled by in slow motion: "Help me . . . Help you . . . Help us . . ."

Dead silence in the auditorium.

Dobb had to double check his notes. "Please welcome Alan . . . Rosenbaum!"

Alan stepped up to his podium, to minimal applause, squinting at the stage glare.

Dobb gestured for Oscar to join him at the podium. "At the Scouts of America, they have a time-honored way of deciding who goes first. Rock, paper, scissors . . ."

The crowd chuckled at this familiar practice.

"I think you know how to play, gentlemen. Fists out," Dobb instructed.

Alan was confused. "Why? Are we fighting?"

Sean rolled his eyes. "Oh my God – you've never played Rock, Paper, Scissors?"

"My parents steered me away from aggressive activities," Alan replied.

Oscar reassured Alan by demonstrating. "It's okay. At the count of three, you choose rock, paper or scissors. Paper covers rock, scissor cuts paper. Rock smashes scissors. Okay, go!"

Alan and Sean did a three count and committed. Sean chose a rock. Alan chose scissors.

"Ha!" Sean exclaimed. "Rock smashes scissors!"

The crowd clapped delightedly.

"Mr. Heston will go first!" Dobb said.

Sean adjusted his microphone and addressed the crowd with the confidence of a local football hero. "Conflict Resolution. That's the theme, to-night? Well, as I look out over this audience, I see a lot of conflicts . . . that got resolved." He spotted a guy in the crowd and addressed him direct-ly. "Hey, Buford, how'd the sale of that property work for ya?"

Buford was a hayseed in the back row. "Great! Once you resolved that little 'zoning' conflict."

The crowd laughed, knowingly.

Sean nodded. "I like helping people in my county. It's what I'm supposed to do." He spotted another guy and asked, "Freddy, that hog farm situation come out all right?"

Freddy was a hog farmer in the front row. "You bet — as soon as you got those greenies out of the way!"

"Conflict resolved!" Sean boasted.

The crowd ate it up.

"It's just how I was raised," Sean explained. "Raised right. Raised in the country. God bless the USA!"

His talk was landing as expected. Applause, bordering on cheers. A little old lady dabbed a tear from her eye with an ornate hankie.

Dobb gestured to Alan, who seemed preoccupied. "And the challenger, Mr. Rosenbaum, your opening statement . . ."

Alan began by pulling a few herbs out of a hemp pouch around his neck and sprinkling them around his podium. Some kids in the crowd giggled.

"That was lavender and sage and oregano to cleanse the negative vibes from my opponent," Alan explained. "And now, a little prayer . . ."

Alan prayed, but it wasn't in English — it was an annoying series of clicks, grunts and whistles.

The little old lady grimaced in disapproval and whispered to a friend, "He's speaking like a savage."

There was a general unease in the room as Alan ended his prayer with harsh breaths and a few loud claps. "Conflict. If conflict never starts . . . it is already resolved."

"Thanks, Confucius!" Sean heckled.

The audience guffawed in agreement.

Alan continued, "The resolution of conflict comes with the dissolution of conflict. Dissolve and resolve."

Zero response, except for Sean. "I call BS! Using violence toward a peaceful end is an American right, just like freedom. No violence, no peace!"

That struck a positive chord with the locals, but Alan challenged him back. "If elected, would you pledge to resolve conflict peaceably?"

"I pledge to resolve conflict *quickly*," Sean replied. "Aggressively. With overwhelming force – and yeah, maybe even violently!"

The crowd clapped at the favorable answer.

Oscar looked to Madison, who shook her head disapprovingly. "This is going nowhere."

"These guys are being D-bags," Oscar added.

"Time for Plan B?"

Oscar nodded in agreement.

"I'm curious. Why not peace as the default and violence as the last resort?" Alan asked.

"Because I happen to find violence very effective," Sean replied, then wound his attentive audience up with, "And if you have a conflict with that, come over here for a resolution!"

The crowd of mostly men leapt to their feet, itching for conflict. Before things could digress beyond shouting, a loud whistle permeated the air.

All eyes fell to fourteen-year-old Scout Oscar, who blew his official Danger Whistle and kept blowing it until the room went silent.

"I'm sorry to interrupt. In the Scouts, we are taught to obey instructions. Neither of you are being civil, *or* constructive," Oscar said.

The crowd generally agreed with that. Oscar looked to Madison, who picked up where he left off. "Oscar and I are one badge away from becoming Eagle Scouts. The Conflict Resolution Badge is earned if you can help two individuals resolve their differences without resorting to violence."

Sean rolled his eyes and said, "Tell you what – I won't punch a hippie today, okay? Badge earned!"

The crowd started to get riled up again, but Oscar blew the shrill whistle again – even louder. "As Scouts, we honor our word by our deeds." He turned to Alan and Sean and asked, "Would you both be willing to submit to the Walk a Mile in My Shoes Challenge? Spend a weekend together in the Oregon desert. Hike together, break bread together, solve problems . . . *together*."

Alan and Sean both reacted like that was a really bad idea, but the crowd buzzed with curiosity.

"At the end of the weekend," Madison added, "each candidate would apply what they learned about working together toward improving their service to this community – regardless of who wins the election."

Locals liked the idea. A smattering of applause.

"Sounds pretty reasonable to me," Dobb said. "Gentlemen? Do you accept?"

"Are you kidding me?" Sean replied. "I survived Desert Storm – I can survive a weekend with a smelly hippie!"

Alan clicked and clapped a few more times. "If I survived Nixon, I can survive this righteous dude!"

The crowd responded with a full-throated cheer. It was on!

IV

THE CHALLENGE

A s Sean packed at home, the atmosphere was tense. Doris was dubious. "A weekend together with what you call 'a smelly hippie.' What exactly are you hoping to get out of this?"

"I'll prove my point," Sean replied.

"What point? That you're out of shape?"

"That I can reach across the aisle – get along with anyone!"

"You can prove that by reaching across the hall – and having an actual conversation with your teenage daughter."

"Apples and oranges," Sean dismissed. "Look, I'm doing this."

"Why?" Doris asked.

"Because I can beat that guy."

"This isn't a competition. You're supposed to work *together.*"

"Oh, I'm gonna pretend to get along with him, sure, but in the end, I have to win."

"Because he's a Democrat," Doris questioned, "or because if you don't, your macho, mostly-male base will think you're slipping."

"Both! Obviously!" Sean snapped. "And honestly, a part of me wants to do this to prove to you that . . . I still got it."

"The only thing you need to prove to me, from time to time, is that I exist."

"What does that mean?"

Doris smiled supportively and kissed Sean on the cheek. "Here's to winning. Don't forget the trick knee."

~

Alan wrapped his packing up. "Don't forget, mom: Ginsy gets wet food Saturday and dry food Sunday. If you feed her wet both days, she'll barf it up."

Esther looked up from her crossword puzzle. "Moses wandered in the desert. You, I'm not so sure about . . ."

"Mother, I am more in tune with the earth than that poser will ever be."

26

"When was the last time you spent the night in a tent?" Esther asked.

". . . At camp . . ."

"When you were ten. Your only hope is to commit murder."

"You can't be serious," Alan said, incredulous.

"Who's gonna know if you 'accidentally' push him off a cliff? Where better to off an adversary than the desert? It's been a mafia staple for decades."

"Mom. I'm going – and nobody is dying."

"Suit yourself," Esther shrugged. "Thank God you wore bright colors. Makes it easier to recover your body."

~

Friends, relatives, Mayor Dobb Dryer and interested town folks were gathered around a crude platform near the trailhead.

The candidates were decked out, with right hands raised. Sean was in his old Desert Storm uniform, and Alan looked very "Lawrence of Arabia."

Scouts Oscar and Madison were leading them in a pledge. "We agree to honor this challenge by completing the entire course as laid out . . ."

Each candidate repeated the words a half beat later.

". . . Working together with the spirit of fairness and honesty. We promise not to cheat," Madison said.

Sean and Alan stole a dubious glance at each other and recited the last words of the oath – neither one thrilled with the verbiage.

Dobb cleared his throat. "All righty, as your Mayor, I hereby declare the Walk a Mile in My Shoes Challenge underway!" The crowd cheered as the candidates stepped down from the podium to the edge of the trail.

Cindy Chan was waiting with her camera. "Gentlemen . . . any final words before you begin what may be a life-changing journey?"

Sean spoke first. "Yes! I'm excited to prove to the people of Dryer County that I can work with anyone – conservatives, Libertarians, The Freeman, Posse Comitatus . . ."

Cindy gestured to Alan. "Even this guy?"

"Well, that's what this challenge is all about, right?" Sean replied. "He'll have to learn to live with a guy who prays before meals and takes a shower every day! That could be his undoing."

Cindy turned her microphone to Alan. "And Mr. Rosenbaum? Think you can work with this man in the Oregon wilderness?"

Alan shrugged and replied, "I'm philosophical. He'll have to get around without a Humvee. That could be a disaster. Forty-eight hours without a Glock strapped to his hip? I'm worried for him. I'm also hoping to not get blisters too badly."

Cindy nodded. "Okay, well, thank you and good luck to you both."

"Only one of us will need it!" Sean assured her.

Cindy signed off as Alan and Sean waved good-byes to well-wishers and headed off, side-by side down the trail.

HOUSE DIVIDED

V

THE JOURNEY

Alan hummed happily as he walked, every so often clapping his hands, or clicking his fingers – like he seemed to do all the time.

"Okay, pal. We're away from the cameras," Sean said. "You can stop all the fake hippie crap now."

Alan shrugged. "That's just sounds of joy, brother. Like breathing or blinking, it's second nature."

"Yeah, well, to a normal person, making random sounds – not in English – is a little creepy." Sean pulled a small, folded map out of his pocket. On it, a crude drawing showed the location of *something*. "But, you know what? I don't really have to deal with you, so go ahead and make all the stupid noises you want." Sean gestured for Alan to go on ahead. "I'll see you at camp."

"You don't want to walk together?" Alan asked, a little thrown by Sean's demeanor.

"Not really."

"You don't think we should . . ."

"No. I don't. This is a photo op," Sean reasoned. "A PR stunt. We are not friends. We are not gonna be friends. What do you hippies say, 'Do your own thing?' So, let's do that. Let's just 'Do our own thing'."

The two men faced each other in uncomfortable silence for a moment.

Eventually, Alan shrugged. "Okay, dude. I guess I'll see ya," and he walked away, slowly down the path.

With Alan out of sight, Sean turned to his right, aligning with a trail mile marker and started counting steps, referring to his "map." "Okay . . ." Sean mumbled to himself, "thirty paces past the five-mile marker, turn left."

Sean paced his steps out then turned to his left, through the underbrush, keeping his map oriented. Still counting, he continued, "Twenty paces in, you will find disturbed earth."

Sure enough, twenty of Sean's paces led him to an area that had indeed been "used." Sean dug with the heel of his boot and connected with a metallic surface. He grinned. "It's nice to have friends . . ."

Sean unearthed an ammunition box full of survival goodies: a night vision scope, emergency c-rations, red bull, flask, hunting knife, satellite phone, gun and numerous rounds of ammo.

".. . in the United States military . . ." Sean unscrewed the cap on his flask and took a long pull.

~

Alan shuffled along, then started eyeing his surroundings, checking for landmarks. Slowly, he pulled a hemp map of his own out of his hemp pants and unfolded it. "Thankfully, a few righteous brothers don't want to see me die in the desert . . ."

Alan turned to his left and saw a rattlesnake skin, wrapped around a thorn bush. He looked back at the map. "Twenty paces east of the rattlesnake skin . . ."

Alan produced a miniature sun dial hanging from a leather strap around his neck. He held it up to the sun to find "east," then proceeded in that direction. "Twenty paces to the Desert Tortoise droppings . . ."

Sure enough, at twenty paces, Alan came across a distinct pile of droppings. "Thank you, brother tortoise," he said, before consulting the map. "Thirty paces south to the Antelope Antlers."

Alan repeated the Sun Dial trick and paced off the remaining steps. He came upon a pair of bleached, discarded antlers and moved it gently aside. "Thank you, brother Antelope . . ."

Underneath, Alan dug out a stash of his own — a hemp-wrapped satchel full of hippie survival goodies. "It's nice to have friends . . ."

Alan shook the desert dust off the bag and revealed a book of edible desert plants, "The Natural Survivalist," a necklace of tokens (which he immediately put on), various restorative balms, herbs (DMT among them) and a dozen beautifully rolled joints.

He cradled the weed. ". . . Loyal hippie friends who think of everything for their brother. First things, first." Alan fired up the doobie and inhaled deeply. "Gotta clear my mind . . ."

VI

DEAD PIONEER RIDGE

Sean and Alan progressed as they made their separate ways across a desert environment that was both desolate and beguiling. Dead Pioneer Ridge was directly ahead.

Each man arrived from different directions and eyed each other warily. There appeared to be only one way over the imposing shelf of rock.

Alan looked at his map. "Dead Pioneer Ridge. Whoa. Yeah. I can see some pioneer dudes dying up there."

Sean walked to the imposing ridge and surveyed the wall that needed to be scaled. "Luckily for me, I did a lot of rock climbing in college. See you on the other side."

Sean spat on his hands and began to ascend the sheer wall, finding impressively small grips along the way. But, before long, he was stymied. The next hold was out of his reach. "Shit."

Alan, who had been trying to find his own way up, got an idea. "Yo! Dude! Stay there!"

"Yeah, thanks," Sean grimaced. "I'm stuck, idiot!"

"No, I know. Stay there – I'm gonna mount you!"

"The hell you are!" Sean said, recoiling.

"Dude – I'll climb your body – to get up to the next grip. Then you climb me. We do that all the way up."

"Uh, that sounds hard . . . and weird . . . but okay, let's try it."

Alan began to "climb" up Sean, using pockets, his belt and different parts as "holds."

"Man, I thought vegans were skinny little things. You weigh a ton," Sean winced.

"Must be the prayer stones . . ." Alan reached into his pockets and pulled out numerous rocks – not small ones! – and tossed them aside.

"You better pray you get up there!" Sean barked.

Alan continued up the man-made, awkward route until he finally got up atop Sean's shoulders. Reaching up, he was close to the next hold, but not close enough. "We're almost there, brother. You cool if I step on your head?"

Sean rolled his eyes. "If it will get you off of me, do what you gotta do!"

"Ok. Hold super still," Alan implored. "If your head wobbles, I'll fall and your cervical vertebrae are toast."

Alan stepped up on Sean's head, spotted the next hold and pushed off mightily – twisting Sean's neck anyway. "What the fuck?" he complained.

Alan got a tenuous hand hold and was able to make his way up to, then over the lip of the ridge. He flopped on his back, sucking air from the exertion, but elated. "Whoo! I made it!"

Sean was still stranded on the sheer face. "Yeah, that worked out pretty well for you, didn't it?"

Alan looked down to Sean. Thinking, he unwound his hemp scarf and started to lower it down. "Climb this, brother."

"Are you kidding? That flimsy thing will never hold me!"

"It's hemp! Pound for pound, it's stronger than steel!"

Sean hesitated, then grabbed the hemp scarf, wrapped it around his wrist and climbed his way up while Alan anchored from above. After much grunting and groaning, Sean made it safely to the windy plateau.

"How about that? Ever thought your life would be saved by hemp?" Alan asked, obviously pleased with himself.

Sean unwrapped the scarf and tossed it back to Alan. "That's a stretch. But thanks."

Alan looked back down the sheer wall. "Okay, so the Scout dudes would be proud."

"How so?"

"We couldn't get up by ourselves, you dig? We had to work together to overcome the obstacle."

Sean looked at Alan, not sharing his joyful moment. "Let's not get all mushy. As far as I'm concerned, if we make it out alive, *none of this* ever happened . . ."

With that, Sean shuffled down the path on his own. "See you at camp."

VII

POISON GULCH

Sean and Alan, still walking separately, made their way across the increasingly harsh terrain.

Sean arrived to see Alan, peering nervously into the imposing chasm over Cripple Creek. There was a "gap" in the trail. "Let me guess: Cripple Creek."

Alan nodded. "Those scout dudes were clever. They knew we'd have to go this way."

"That's a wicked gap. Long jump was not my best event. Got any ideas?"

"Yoga."

"Yoga. You're gonna do that right now?" Sean asked, annoyed.

Alan walked to the gap and sized it up. "Totally! I'll do a 'plank' across the gap. I'll be the bridge and you walk across me."

Sean looked at the gap and the distance below. "Boy, I dunno. Not a lot of room for error."

"I got this," Alan assured, as he raised his arms above his head, inhaled deeply and recited: "I am the Bridge Over Troubled Waters. I will be straight and true!"

Alan fell forward in a dead drop and sure enough, his stretched-out body plugged the gap perfectly. "Move quickly, brother!" Alan urged, straining like mad. "I'm feeling that old hernia operation!"

Sean gulped. "Did I mention I have a trick knee?" Then, he was off, "walking" across Alan. It was a wobbly, dangerous path. The men whispered dueling mantras.

"Come on knee, come on knee . . ."

"Come on hernia, come on hernia . . ."

Sean got to the other side without incident and turned back toward Alan, who released his feet and now dangled from his hands. "Okay, brother. Help me up!"

Sean bent down, took Alan by the hands and began to back up. That's when his right knee – his trick knee – made a subtle "click" sound, which sent him collapsing to the dirt. "Crap! My knee! I can't pull anymore!" he cried.

Sean's grip wouldn't last forever either.

Alan had to think fast. As he scanned the area, he saw a majestic big horn sheep, staring intently down at them. Alan called out, "Mother sheep!"

The sheep looked quizzically at Alan and bleated.

"We need your strength! Hear our pleas!" Alan begged.

"Stop yelling at the sheep you stupid hippie!" Sean barked. "You're just gonna piss it off!"

Alan was undeterred and continued, "BLAAH! BLAAH!"

The sheep looked at Alan, then slowly made its way down the craggy rock face toward them – mind you, it looked like the sheep, big horns and all, was heading right toward Sean's protruding backside!

"What are you doing?," Sean asked, mortified. "That thing is gonna head butt me in the ass, then I'm gonna head butt you, then we're both gonna head butt the bottom of the canyon!"

"Do not fear what you do not understand!" Alan replied.

The sheep, in fact, did not had butt Sean. Instead, it grabbed the back of Sean's tactical belt with its teeth and began to back away from the edge, taking Sean and Alan with it.

"It's working!" Alan continued. "Pull, Mother Sheep! BLAAAAHHH!"

The sheep dug in. After much straining and bleating, Sean and Alan were pulled to safety. The sheep let go of Sean's belt and majestically walked away.

The men collapsed on the ground in stunned silence.

Alan offered a handshake. "Promise me right now, you're never hunting the brother bighorn sheep again."

Sean took his hand and they shook aggressively. "Deal."

VIII

CRIPPLE CREEK

Sean and Alan, now walking together, continued the arduous journey to the next crossing.

Our heroes came to the edge of Cripple Creek, a fast-moving river that wasn't a creek at all – it was a raging torrent.

"Cripple Creek?! I wouldn't exactly call that a creek!" Sean said, exasperated.

Alan consulted the map. "That's what it says. Maybe to the pioneer dudes, this wasn't such a big deal."

Alan spotted an old mining bucket, connected to a rusty cable that stretched across the river to a crumbling receiving station – all worthy of a Western Heritage museum.

Alan pointed downstream. "There's your crossing."

"Are you kidding?" Sean asked. "That shit hasn't been used since the Civil War."

The men walked over to the cable rig and inspected it. Structural integrity: compromised.

"Okay, look, I'll go first," Alan said. "It's simple: I get in the bucket, you pull the cable, I go across, send the bucket back, pull you across. It'll be dope."

Alan climbed into the bucket as Sean handled the cable.

"It looks rickety as shit. Be ready for anything!" Sean warned.

"I'm ready! Pull!"

Sean yanked on the crusty cable, which fed through a well-worn turnbuckle, but the bucket didn't move an inch.

"Must be a two-man job!" Alan shouted. "Get in!"

Sean joined Alan in the bucket and it swayed precariously. The men grabbed the cable together and heaved. This time, the bucket lurched forward toward the river, albeit haltingly.

They reached the edge of the churning water. Falling in at this point would not be good.

"We're killin' it! Keep going!" Alan encouraged.

Sean and Alan, sweating up a storm, fed the rusted, decaying cable through their hands. Soon, they were directly over the rapids. The cable creaked, the bucket rattled and the wood infrastructure began to split.

"We got it!" Alan shouted.

Sproing! A cable connector snapped.

"I'm not so sure about that!" Sean looked down to see a horrifying whirlpool directly below. "Pull faster!"

"Doin' the best I can, brother!"

"Stop calling me that!"

Then – Pow! Creak! GROOOAAANNN! Their bucket plummeted toward the river. Instinctively, Alan handed Sean a freed feeder cable, not connected to the bucket. "Quick! Hold this cable!" Alan said, urgently.

"Why? Are you a structural engineer?"

"Yes!"

With that, because of the angle of descent and the tension of the feeder cable, Sean was whisked out of the bucket while Alan rode it crashing down into the river.

Sean landed, swinging on the cable a la Tarzan, along the shore on the opposite side of the river. He saw Alan thrashing in the rapids – his hemp scarf now drowning him in weight and bulk.

Sean raced along the shore, shedding unnecessary gear as he went, then swan dove headfirst into the into the frothing rapids.

In the chaos of the river, Sean swam up to Alan with powerful strokes and hooked an elbow under his chin, classic rescue style.

"Don't worry, Alan, all rapids end eventually," Sean shouted above the roar. "Keep your head above water and watch for the eddy up ahead!"

Alan reacted quizzically to Sean's statement. "That's the first time you ever called me by my name!"

With that, they were both swept away in the ferocious rapid.

Sure enough, men, gear and equipment were all vomited out at the next eddy. Sean and Alan swam for the shore and collapsed on dry ground.

"So, you really were a structural engineer?" Sean asked.

Alan nodded. "UC Berkeley."

"Why'd you give it up?"

". . . Too structured."

Both men shared a dark laugh.

"Well, that was pretty selfless for a hippie," Sean admitted.

Alan looked to the river, then back to Sean. "I probably would have drown back there. Where'd you learn to swim like that?"

"High School. We beat Klamath Falls for the state champs. It was a big deal."

"Well, that was pretty selfless for a hippie hater."

There was a quiet moment between them – perhaps the first one, minus the pretense and contempt.

Eventually, Sean stood up and squinted into the blazing sun. "Let's get to camp."

IX

THISTLE MEADOW

Sean and Alan dragged themselves to the "Camp" marker along the trail. They were mud-caked and sun-beaten, but alive.

Sean surveyed the area and glanced at his tactical watch. "Okay, so I'm sure you're not real keen on manual labor, but before the sun goes down, we have to make camp."

"Fear not, Brother Sean, Alan replied. "I always carry my load. According to the Scout rules, we have to do it together anyway."

Sean let out a heavy sigh. "Fine. It'll get done quicker that way. Let's do the tent first."

Sean dumped the communal tent out and plastic stakes rolled across the desert dust.

Alan scratched his head. "Should we read the instructions? The ones the Scouts left?"

"It's a stupid tent," Sean said, with a dismissive wave. "It'll take two seconds. First, you unfold the rod-thingies."

Alan picked up a folded rod and it straightened instantly – whack! – right into Sean's face.

Swatting it away, Sean grumbled, "You obviously haven't camped much." Then, he unfolded the other rod directly into his own crotch – whang!

Alan stifled a laugh. "Obviously not, brother Sean."

The guys eventually read the instructions and stumbled through the process, with a lot of bickering and mistakes along the way.

~

Well into meal preparations, Sean flipped a Fred Flintstone size steak and Alan returned from the nearby woods with fresh herbs, nuts and flowers for the salad.

Sean glanced at Alan's haul. "What makes you think I'm gonna eat that rabbit food?"

"You'll need it to push half a cow through your intestinal tract," Alan replied. "Dandelions are a great source of fiber."

"I'll stay paleo, thanks."

"Dude. We took an oath. We're supposed to share."

"Are you telling me you're gonna eat some of this steak?" Sean challenged.

"I'm willing to try it."

Sean cut off a corner of the steak and put it on Alan's plate. "Ok. I'll try your rabbit food and you can try my real food."

Alan recoiled at the bloody steak. "The smell of captivity, torture and death is enough to make me vomit."

"Hey, you wanted to play by the rules. Try it!"

Alan put the charred meat in his mouth and chewed slowly. It was not an unpleasant experience. "Whoa. That's really savory – and really TASTY!"

Sean laughed heartily. "See? It didn't kill you! You need protein in that bony ass body of yours."

Alan held a bowl and camp fork out to Sean. "Your turn. Vegetables. Raw. As nature intended. A little salt, pepper and walnut oil doesn't hurt either."

Sean wrinkled his nose, but he took a fork full of greens and chowed down. After some protracted chewing, he cracked a smile. "Okay . . . okay . . . not bad. Kinda sweet. Not bitter at all."

Alan enjoyed this immensely. "See? It didn't kill you! You need vegetables in that bulky body of yours."

The two men chuckled and proceeded to eat each other's meal.

After a few more bites, Sean produced his flask. "When you say share, I guess you mean . . . everything." He took a long pull off his flask and held it out. "Share my whiskey."

Alan pulled out a beautiful joint. "Share and share alike?"

Sean nodded. "I'll do yours if you do mine."

Alan shrugged and took the flask from Sean. He pursed his lips and took a pull. He immediately began to cough like he had been poisoned. "This is the foulest liquid in the universe!"

Alan fired up his doobie, got it primed and passed it to Sean.

"The gateway drug," Sean muttered. "Ok. Here goes . . ." He puffed on the joint like it was a cigarette and immediately coughed uncontrollably. "Wow. Okay, my lungs are permanently damaged."

"It's not a toxic cigarette, dude," Alan explained. "No need to blow it out right away. You gotta hold it in your lungs. Let it linger. Get high."

Sean tried again and took a huge hit, holding it in as long as possible.

"That's the idea!" Alan said, approvingly.

Sean eventually exhaled a huge plume of smoke. "Okay, now what?"

Alan shrugged. "Now you wait. Maybe five minutes."

"Ok," Sean Said, studying Alan. "How do *you* feel?"

"I kind of have a warm glow in my belly. Let me try that again."

Sean passed the flask and Alan had a more "successful" pull this time. "It's like drinking golden tree sap with powerful juju."

Sean took another hit off the joint. "It's like a stinky old cigar . . . only . . . *different* . . ." As soon as Sean said the word, he realized that he was stoned. Really stoned. "Whoa . . ."

Alan looked at Sean. The booze was starting to work its magic on him. "Whoa . . ."

After a contracted pause, both men made eye contact and immediately burst into hysterical laughter.

"You know, I normally hate radicals. But somehow, you seem okay," Sean conceded.

Alan smiled and shrugged. "I love breathing air that you can't see. That doesn't make me a radical."

"All you enviro freaks want to lock up the land."

"That's because your idea of a wilderness experience includes motorized vehicles, alcohol and guns."

Sean winked, producing a handgun. "Don't knock it 'til you've tried it!"

Alan just about fell off his stump. "Whoa. Dude. That's a . . . *gun*," he said, with a combination of fear and dread.

"Beretta 92F. Try it."

Alan held up his hands. "Oh, I don't *do* guns."

"C'mon," Sean goaded. "You want to understand me? Shoot a gun."

"But I've never shot one in my life!" Alan exclaimed.

"Just do it once. What was the saying about walking in the other guy's shoes?"

Alan shakes his head, ruefully. "Shoes are one thing, brother. A handgun is another."

Sean spun the Beretta on the end of his finger. "It's registered, if that makes you feel any better. I didn't even buy it at a gun show."

Alan exhaled. He was deeply conflicted, but deeply curious. "Okay. I'll shoot one shot. But *that's it.*"

Sean loaded one bullet into the clip and chambered the round. "No prob." He spun the gun around and held it out.

Alan took it slowly, hesitantly. "Whoa. It's heavy. And *cold.*"

"Your palm will warm it up."

Alan looked around. "What should I shoot?"

Sean took a plastic cup, filled it with sand and placed it atop a fairly level stump. "Let's see if you can hit that cup."

Alan swung the gun over, straightened his arm and closed and eye. "I can't see anything."

"Close the other eye."

Alan switched eyes and that seemed to work better.

"Just squeeze the trigger," Sean coaxed. "Let the gun do the work."

Click. Nothing.

"Take the safety off first."

Alan looked closer at the gun. "Where is it?"

Sean pointed out the small, round button and Alan flipped it off. "That's a good feature," he admitted.

Sean nodded in full agreement. "Yeah, it's great when amateurs handle weapons."

Alan took aim again and squeezed the trigger. BOOM! The bullet splintered the cup, sending a fountain of sand into the air.

"Whoooh!," Alan shouted. "Dude, that was awesome. It really has a kick. You see that? Pretty good shot."

Sean clapped approvingly. "Damn good. Okay, let me have it back. Your one shot is done."

But Alan pulled the gun away. "Dude. Wait. Maybe just one more . . ."

~

More weed was smoked, more liquor consumed as Alan and Sean proceeded to blow the living crap out of every random thing in camp. Finally, in a flourish, Alan emptied his entire clip into a pine cone, spinning it back and forth across the campground with each well-placed shot. Click! He was finally out of ammo.

Puffing on a massive spliff, Sean applauded. "Whoo! Dead eye Dick! If I didn't know better, I'd think you had a knack for guns."

Alan took the joint out of Sean's hand. "If I didn't know better, I'd say you had stoner written all over you."

Sean laughed. "Ha!"

Alan laughed too. "Ha!"

Sean wobbled to his feet. "Okay, time to hit the hay. Sure you want to go through with this?"

"We said we would try."

Sean looked at the cramped tent. "Which side do you want?"

"Well, I sleep on my left, so . . . if I sleep on the right, I'll face away from you."

Sean shrugged. "All the same to me. I sleep on my back. Full disclosure: I have been told that I snore."

Alan nodded. "Full disclosure: I have been told that my farts, which are part of any natural digestive process, are rather . . . ripe."

"Great. Maybe we'll cancel each other out."

Alan and Sean got situated in the tent.

Sean laid on his back and folded his hands across his chest. "Okay, look, you can do what you want, but I say my prayers before bed."

"Out loud?"

Sean looked at Alan. "Yeah. I've always done it that way."

"Ok. Cool. I, too, have nighttime offerings that I make. Out loud."

"Okay. We probably should take turns. You want to go first?" Sean inquired.

"No, you go, dude. I'll follow your lead."

Sean closed his eyes and clasped his hands tightly. "Heavenly father, I thank you for today. For protecting me – uh, us . . . through our ordeals and I pray for safe passage tomorrow. Thanks to Jesus Christ our lord and savior that we overcome our sins and make recompense. Amen."

"Amen. That was pretty tame," Alan said, smiling.

"That was the short version."

"I agreed with most of it," Alan offered. "I get a little distracted around the baby Jesus part, but all good."

Sean gestured to Alan. "Your turn."

Alan sat up and crossed his legs. He made a few sounds like he was clearing his nostrils and began to clap and click randomly. "Great spirit, I . . . *we* . . . rise up to meet you! To greet you!"

Click! Clap!

"We rise to be one with your spirit!"

Clap! Click! Clap!

"Protect us. Away darkness, away temporal, away earth!"

Two more clicks and Alan wrapped up his offering by emitting a long hiss.

"Not so bad," Sean admitted. "The clapping thing is a little fruity, but I expected worse."

"This is totally good, dude. We're sharing our thing. Walking in each other's moccasins."

Sean rolled away from Alan, adjusting his sleeping bag. "With all due respect, I won't be walking in yours. You and I are farther apart than the gap at Cripple Creek Canyon. But at least we're trying. Good night."

"Peace out, dude."

The men assumed their respective positions as advertised and began to fall asleep.

Then . . . SNOOOOORRRR – Sean let out a rattler.

Alan immediately bolted awake. "Dude, that is so bogus."

But Sean didn't even hear. He was too busy calving epic snores into the small tent. Alan turned away, pulled the covers over his head and – FAAAARRRRRTTTT! let one rip.

It took a moment to sink in, but the smell was enough to wake Sean up. "Oh, my God! What is that horrible stench?"

"It's just biology, friend."

"It smells like a dead body!"

FAAAAARRRRRRTTTT! Alan let another one go and that was one too many for Sean. He grabbed his sleeping bag, a few other items and bolted out of the tent. "The scouts never said we had to endure torture on a primordial level. You and your Brewer's Yeast are spooning alone tonight, pal – I'm outta here!" Sean waved at the air in front of his face. "If that's the result of being 'all natural,' I'll take processed any day of the week!"

Alan responded with another epic FAAARRRRTTT!

"Sweet Jesus," Sean muttered.

~

Sean bedded down safely away and set up his sleeping bag. Within minutes, he was flat on his back, executing the perfect "dead man's snore."

What neither of the men realized was that a decent sized black bear was lurking nearby – lured by the smell of cooked meat. The bear licked the pan Sean had used, then made its way to the tent Alan was in.

The bear poked its snout inside – just in time for another FAAARRRT! The startled bear withdrew sharply and stumbled away, dangerously close to Sean, who was snoring through it all.

The bear hunched over and started to grunt. An enormous, berry-riddled bear crap dropped to the desert floor about a foot from Sean's snoring face. "Man, your farts smell even worse over here," he complained, sleepily. "You need to move downwind from me – over *there*."

As Sean pointed, he opened his eyes to reveal not only the pile of steaming bear crap – but the bear itself! Sean screamed at the top of his lungs, "BEAR!!!!" and leapt out of his bag, shedding it like a cocoon. He dove into the open flap of the flimsy tent with such force, the entire thing rolled down the nearest hill.

Alan shouted amid the chaos of plunging down the slope. "I don't see any bear!"

Sean was slashing about with his utility knife, cutting irreparable gashes in the tent as gear bounced in every direction, flying out of the new holes. "That's because it's right on top of us!"

Up the hill, the bear watched the disaster unfold from a safe distance as the mess came crashing to a halt. Sean popped his head out of a new slash in the fabric, only to see the bear slowly sauntering away. "Thank God! My quick thinking saved us!"

Alan poked his head out next to him, completely disheveled. ". . . Or not."

~

Day broke in this austere, pristine wilderness – pristine except for the garbage bomb that went off after a night of weed, booze, guns and animal interaction.

Alan was sound asleep in his bag – a makeshift turban wrapped around his head to protect from the intrusions of light and sound.

Sean also slept outside in his bag, snoring loudly and happily as the first rays of light streaked across the land. As Sean leaned his head to one side, a scorpion was revealed, crawling up the side of his face! Thinking he was dreaming, Sean mumbled, "Huh. Tickles. Stop it, sweetie. I want to sleep, I . . ."

WHACK! A rock hit Sean square on the temple, smashing the scorpion in the process.

Sean grabbed his head in agony. "Ow! Son of a bitch!" He wobbled to his feet, stunned. He looked to see Alan nearby, clearly the one who chucked the rock.

"Sorry, dude, brother scorpion was about to strike," he explained. "I had to think fast."

"Which is worse?" Sean asked, rubbing his temple, "A scorpion sting or a Grade 3 concussion?"

"Well, there's good news, friend — all we have to do is get back to the rendezvous point, shake a few hands and we can move on with our lives."

"You're right," Sean agreed. "After all we've been through, the rest is cake!"

HOUSE DIVIDED

X

CRIPPLE CREEK REDUX

Sean and Alan made their way along the return trail and came to the edge of Cripple Creek. Sean looked at the creek and rattled his near-empty canteen. "Gotta hydrate!"

The guys made their way down to the edge of the river. As they refueled, a sound caught their attention — a consistent, unpleasant, motorized sound, coming from upstream.

Alan tilted his head as he listened. "Is that a fucking engine? In the fucking wilderness?"

They followed the sound to a bend in the tributary, which revealed a motorized dredge on the riverbank, puttering away, powering a dredge belt.

Alan pointed at the rig with an accusing finger. "Mining in the middle of nowhere? Dude. Are you kidding me?"

Sean waved it off. "Big deal. There are private inholdings everywhere back here."

The camp didn't seem inhabited at the moment.

Sean was getting anxious. "C'mon, let's go. Before someone comes back. Out here, People are touchy about their stuff."

"No, brother Sean," Alan protested. "This doesn't feel right. I can't abide. I have to do something."

"Suit yourself," Sean said, turning away. "I'm not getting a load of buckshot over a mining claim. See you at the rendezvous."

Ignoring Sean, Alan crept closer, under cover of the brush along the banks, scanning the trashed, primitive campsite. "SO bogus!" he growled.

Alan spotted a toolbox, bursting with industrial-sized wrenches and screwdrivers. He slid out a large monkey wrench and weighed it in his hand. "This is for you, Mother."

With a last, nervous look around, Alan raced up to the small engine and smashed the wrench on the carburetor, ruining it. It was so easy, Alan took a whack at the dredge belt mechanism and destroyed that too. The area fell silent, except for the sound of wind through the trees.

"Ahhh, finally – the sound of the *wild* . . ." Alan mused, inhaling deeply.

Then, behind him – CLICK-CLACK-RACK – the sound of automatic weapons chambering rounds.

Alan whirled around to see Pit Bull, a full-on desert-style biker, flanked by two gnarly dudes – all armed to the teeth, with AR-15s pointed directly at him.

Pit Bull grinned, exposing a handful of missing teeth. ". . . The *wild west*, maybe . . ."

Alan gulped.

HOUSE DIVIDED

XI

ECOTOPIA

Sean walked along the trail, oblivious to Alan's fate, enjoying the solitude until a faint sound caught his attention. He stopped to listen. The sound happened again – like a soft, woody instrument blowing a melodic tune.

"Is that a lute?" Sean asked himself, as he followed the sound away from the trail, along the river. The musical sound grew louder, but still seemed far away. Sean moved along an elevated ridge with a perfect view down to the river. The sound grew more distinct – a solemn, yet joyful tune.

At a sharp bend up ahead, Sean stopped cold. In the distance, a group of colorful hippies were engaged in some sort of ritual.

Sean frowned. "Hippies. Gross." He pulled out his binoculars. Upon closer inspection, the hippies all appeared to be women. They were gathered under a large, rustic gazebo, decked out with flowers and ribbons and flags of all colors. "At least they're women."

Sean focused his binoculars on two women, proceeding slowly down a makeshift aisle, holding hands. They were a tanned, revealingly clad, stunning couple – a hippie magazine cover shot.

The hippie couple in question was surrounded by friends, supporters and Evenki, a hippie Shaman, leading the ceremony. "This blessed day," Evenki intoned, "We welcome you all to Ecotopia . . ."

Sean rolled his eyes. "Oh boy. Calling Fantasy Island . . ."

"We are here to join the spirits of two beings – into one," Evenki continued. She gestured to the more mature hippie woman, Brigid. She was forty-something, confident and beaming on this day. "Brigid, the exalted one, triple goddess – maiden, mother, wise. Do you take the hand of Eos, goddess of the dawn, as your life partner . . . ?"

Evenki swept her hand to Eos, a classic "flower child," also buoyantly beautiful – albeit twenty years younger than Brigid. ". . . To cherish and nurture the feminine side of each other so you may find the wholeness that is the true woman within?"

Sean raised an eyebrow. "A hippie *wedding*? And a May/December, gender bender wedding to boot! God save my soul!"

Brigid smiled unabashedly. "I do!"

Evenki turned to Eos. "Do you, Eos, take the hand of Brigid as the woman to fulfill your spiritual and feminine quest to be free of male influence and dominance?"

Eos lit up. "I do!"

The women at the ceremony erupted into spontaneous shouts of support.

Evenki raised her arms. "I now pronounce you, goddess to goddess, a union of one. You may kiss!"

Brigid and Eos engaged in an extended kiss. The crowd celebrated with whoops and hugs.

Sean looked closer with the binoculars, not exactly hating what he witnessed. "Nothing wrong with a group of young people engaging in a spiritual activity . . ." He craned his neck for a better view, when – CLICK – Sean's right knee – the trick one – made that little sound. "Uh-Oh. My trick kneeeeee –" And with that, Sean careened down the craggy hillside toward the river. "Wha–haaaa!!!"

The applauding hippies all turned their attention to the commotion in time to see Sean bite it badly down the rocky slope – BAM! CRACK! SMACK! – landing face down in the river! His inert body began to drift in the current toward the women at the ceremony.

Bast, goddess of warfare, with cat-like looks and design – stepped forward for a better look. "It's a man."

The women watched Sean float, like he was a dead alien.

Bast turned to Brigid, who was the elder of the group. "Should we help him?"

Kuan Yin, the goddess of mercy, stepped forward. She looked mean and tough, but her speech was always wise and peaceful. She also looked to Brigid. "He is a man, but he is also a fellow human in peril. We must help him."

Brigid, who was a pragmatist in her own way, nodded. "I agree. No man is dying in Ecotopia today. Grab him, sisters!"

The hippies splashed into the river and fished Sean out. They deposited him, sputtering, on the shore.

Brigid approached. She was the clear leader of the group as well as the blushing bride. "Roll him over."

Several women rolled Sean over on his back. He spat out the last of the silty river water.

"Can you speak?" Brigid asked.

"I . . . lost my footing . . . out hiking . . ." Sean replied.

"Copping a perv more like it, old man," Brigid accused. You know you're trespassing."

"I'm not so sure about that, Flower Child . . ."

Bast and a few other women began to circle Sean, threateningly. He struggled to get up. "Hey, I'm not looking for any trouble. I just want to get back to where I came from."

"Good," Brigid agreed. "Leave. The sooner the better."

"Fine by me." Sean took one step and fell on his face. "Okay, maybe not. I have a trick knee. I can't put any weight on it. Can I get a ride to town?"

"We don't own a car," Brigid replied flatly.

"Right. You're hippies."

Brigid circled the women for a talk. She took Eos's hand. "Surely, the goddess of love has tested us today, but we must not let her down. We will deal with this negative male energy and get back to our blessed selves. This is a test. We shall endure and overcome."

Brigid addressed Sean. "You may stay with us until you are able to leave. Until then, we will care for you like one of our own."

All eyes of the women fell to Sean, who held his knee gingerly. "Cool. Appreciate it. Hey, uh, do hippies do pain killers?"

HOUSE DIVIDED

DRYER DESERT TRAIL

DEAD PIONEER RIDGE 3
POISON GULCH 8
CRIPPLE CREEK 11
THISTLE MEADOW 13

XII

TRAILHEAD

Local boosters – basically the same ones from before – were putting the finishing touches on podiums and platforms. A Geek Squad guy was stringing microphone wire.

Cindy Chan from KDRY stood by, checking her equipment.

Dobb Dryer was making small talk with Oscar and Madison, the intrepid Scouts. "I sure am excited for you Scouts. It looks like that Conflict Resolution Badge is in the bag!" Dobb paused before admitting, "Golly, I didn't amount to a hill of beans when I was your age . . ."

Three hours later, the same group was now mostly dissipated, with devoted stragglers fanning themselves in the afternoon heat.

A concerned Dobb approached Oscar and Madison as he eyed his watch. "Well, I'm afraid our candidates have missed the deadline. They could be lost."

Oscar stepped forward. "It's our route. The Scouts laid it out. We know the way. Madison and I will go find them."

Cindy perked up. "Not without me."

"You're just a girl," Oscar objected.

Madison swatted him on the shoulder. "So am I, dufus!"

"Not just a girl," Cindy clarified. "KDRY's live on the scene Cindy Chan. I'll go where you won't. *Embed* me."

Confused, Oscar asked, "Like . . . in the military?"

"Something like that."

"Well, either way, you'd best be off," Dobb urged. "Time's a wastin'."

The Scouts shouldered their gear and headed off – with Cindy in tow – on this important mission.

~

Alan found himself cuffed to a side car of a motorcycle being driven by Pit Bull, one of the gnarly dudes. They were being escorted by a handful of other gnarly dudes on gnarly vehicles down a gnarly, rutted road.

Alan was scared, but ever-inquisitive. "Dude, I feel like I'm in a *Mad Max* movie. Where are you taking me?"

"To Cascadia," Pit Bull responded.

"Never heard of it."

"You will."

HOUSE DIVIDED

XIII

THE CRIPPLE CREEK RANCH

A stately entrance of stone and wrought iron. The Cripple Creek Ranch was a masterfully built, turn-of-the-century compound designed for someone with money. Two iron Cs were mounted at the crest of the gate, representing the original ranch logo. A new-ish, floral sign hung beneath: *Ecotopia*.

A hippy girl walked barefoot under the massive, gated entrance toward the main ranch house. She waved at other hippie women going about their business in Ecotopia.

Sean woke up, slowly. He was in an old ranch house room with sandstone walls, high ceilings and hand-hewn beams. He was lying prone in a wooden wheelchair, his leg elevated on a wobbly support. His clothes had been swapped out for desert hippie wear – hemp shirt, pants and sandals.

A voice emanated from across the room: "How do you feel?"

Sean looked up to see Evenki, the Shaman, smiling down at him.

"Like I've been transported to another planet," he said. "But my knee feels fine. What did you put on it?"

"Turmeric root. For inflammation. We also gave you some Diaeme."

"Diaeme. What's that?"

"A plant. To help you 'separate.'"

"Why would I want to do that?"

"To divorce yourself from the pain of your injury," Evenki elaborated, "so you can look back at it objectively and fearlessly."

Sean looked at his knee. "Yeah, I'm pretty separated. Am I . . . tripping?"

"There are many names for it."

Realizing that he was, for the first time, having a hallucinatory experience, Sean freaked out. "Holy schmoly, I'm gonna get hollered at!"

Brigid, Eos and Maia entered.

"I hope Mr. Heston is feeling better," Brigid said.

"Normally, I wouldn't be caught dead in a hippie compound," Sean replied, "but this Dy-May crap is makin' me pretty agreeable."

"Maia, let's show Mr. Heston what we do here."

Brigid led the way as Maia wheeled Sean outside. "Hey, cool ride!"

HOUSE DIVIDED

XIV

WELCOME TO CASCADIA

Alan and the cavalcade of odd vehicles rolled into the former mining town of Crump, Oregon – former, because it was now a falling-down ghost town. A shoddy, "Welcome to Cascadia" wooden plank sign had been nailed over the original.

Crump was oddly untouched – a City Hall, Saloon, Jail, Courthouse, Boarding house and Dry Goods store were all still standing, albeit leaning and gray.

The side car pulled in front of the "jail."

Alan glanced at Pit Bull's rig. "I have to say, dude, kidnapping aside, sweet ride!"

Pit Bull turned his bike off. "Appreciate it. Took a shit ton of welding."

Pit Bull was the Lieutenant Governor of Cascadia, which meant he was more or less the Governor's enforcer. He was also the Director of Maintenance, producing an enormous ring of antique keys as he escorted Alan inside.

Alan was manhandled toward a cell in this time capsule of a frontier jail, but he balked. "Whoa. Ok, dude, if we're talking incarceration here, I gotta lawyer up or whatever the term is."

Pit Bull unlocked the rusty door. CREEAAAK! "All you 'gotta do' is get in there and shut your mouth."

Slam! Pit Bull locked Alan in the skanky, but functional cell and turned to his men on the way out. "Get the Governor."

XV

THE GRAND TOUR

Sean was wheeled about on a tour of the compound and it couldn't had been more inviting. A soothing breeze made everything come alive. Ancient trees dominated the manicured grounds and the dappled light was intoxicating.

Brigid led the way, sharing the history along with Eos and Maia, who steered the rickety wheelchair. "This started as a mining claim in the 1860's, then a ranch my great-grandfather ran – the Cripple Creek," she explained. "My parents quit ranching, so it passed to me. I don't eat meat, so no need for cattle. Now, it's a retreat."

Sean looked up at her, quizzically. "What are you retreating from?"

"The same thing you are when you drink beer and go hunting in the mountains for bighorn sheep."

Sean held up a palm. "I promised never to do that again . . . *hunt*, that is."

"We're all gathered here to enjoy life the way it used to be," Brigid elaborated. "Simple. We might have that in common – minus the guns, the murder and the meat."

The group rounded a corner to reveal an enormous greenhouse, fully operational. A team of hippie women oversaw the massive grow-op of at least 100 marijuana plants, plus an array of herbs and vegetables.

Sean took in the enormous undertaking. "If there was a hippie heaven, this would be it!"

Brigid smiled at Maia. "As the goddess of Growth and Increase, this is Maia's domain."

Maia smiled shyly. "We have created a self-sustaining, biodynamic closed loop – living in subservience to the land, not in domination of it."

"That might be hard for a man to understand," Brigid added.

Sean begged to differ. "I think the herbal Diaeme stuff is helping . . . a lot . . . because I think I almost understood what you just said."

The group passed elevated cables, with dozens of plants hanging to dry. Maia noticed that Sean couldn't take his eyes off the mountain of weed. "Would you like to sample some of the latest harvest?"

"Well, as a guest, I'd hate to be rude . . ." Sean replied.

Maia smiled. A hippie woman offered up a freshly rolled joint. Maia lit it, inhaled heartily and passed it to Sean. Without hesitation, he sucked down a lung full of THC and promptly coughed his brains out.

"Good shit."

HOUSE DIVIDED

XVI

FRONTIER JUSTICE

The raised mahogany judge's bench, still in one piece, loomed over the proceedings. Pit Bull led Alan to a worn, wooden chair on the witness stand in this ancient courthouse.

Pit Bull cleared his throat and stood erect. "All rise for the Honorable Karl Kessler!"

There were only a few people in the courtroom, but they all rose. Pit Bull opened a door for Judge Karl Kessler. He was ancient and crabby. After a slow-motion walk, often with Pit Bull at his elbow, the Judge took his place behind the bench and slammed his gavel. "Proceed!"

Pit Bull opened another door. Governor Ken Johnson and his Attorney General Maury Podnik entered. They were a contrast of looks and style. Ken Johnson was a round, squat little fellow. He was the Governor of Cascadia – and quite the know-it-all. Maury was a tall, lean, almost crow-like "Lawyer" for Cascadia. He carried a Book of Statutes and whispered a lot.

Ken Johnson took a moment conferring with Maury and their stack of paperwork, then turned dramatically toward the bench. "Thank you, your honor. This is a sad day for Cascadia. Today, we have to deal with not only an interloper, but a saboteur."

Alan raised his hand.

Judge Karl eyed him. "Whaddya want?"

"Your honor, like, what am I being accused of?"

The Judge looked at his notes. "You're on the hook for trespassing, vandalism, criminal mischief . . ."

Alan was incredulous. "I object! This is the Owyhee Wilderness. Federally designated. How is trespassing even possible, bro?"

Ken Johnson stood in defiance. "Map!"

Pit Bull rolled over a large Oregon map, push-pinned into a cork board. Ken Johnson approached and gestured to a new border, drawn in red sharpie, encompassing northern California and about a third of the lower part of Oregon – including Dryer County. "Your honor, I present the State of Jefferson, Republic of the Pacific."

Maury found the statute and added, "As defined by Land Appropriation Statute 2016-02C."

Alan struggled to understand. "What does that even mean?"

Bang! The Judge's gavel rattled the bench. "Trespassing charge so stands!"

Ken Johnson addressed the court. "Your honor, the accused also ruined $5,280 worth of mining equipment."

Maury handed over some paperwork. "Receipts herein entered into the record."

"I object your honor!" Alan shouted. "The mining operation is there totally illegally! I can't be charged for wrecking something that's not supposed to be there!"

Judge Karl considered this for a moment. "Good point. Objection sustained."

"You honor, our mining operation, as you know, is the life blood of Cascadia . . ." Ken Johnson pointed out, with a knowing look to the judge, "Including municipal salaries."

The judge immediately changed his tune. "Objection overruled. The Vandalism and Criminal mischief charges stand!"

Alan stood up, outraged. "Totally bogus, dude!"

Pit Bull grabbed Alan by the scruff of his neck and shoved him back in his chair. "Shuddup!"

Ken Johnson sorted through some papers. "We have also calculated the loss of earnings since the wanton destruction of property."

Maury handed a document to the judge, who raised his eyebrows and emitted a low whistle. "Losses to Cascadia amount to $87,000 . . . plus existing damages."

Alan was gob smacked. "Your honor, I'm a self-help guru. I pull in about twenty-five grand a year – and that's if I don't offer any discounted treatment packages. I'll never pay that back – I'll die in the mines!"

"Quite possibly. Sentencing tomorrow around noon," concluded the Judge. "No earlier. I feel a bender coming on."

Alan rose back to his feet. "Surely, the good citizens of Cascadia would be open to barter as a means to pay off a debt to the state. Is that in the statutes?"

Judge Karl looked to Maury. "Is it?"

Maury consulted the Book of Statutes. "It is."

"What do you have in mind?" Judge Karl queried.

"Pot, your honor. Lots of it. A grow-op the size of a football field. I'm entitled to half of it in a divorce settlement. I offer that as barter to settle this."

Judge Karl looked to Ken Johnson. "Ken Johnson, what say ye?"

Ken Johnson waffled. "Well, if the alleged marijuana can be verified, your honor . . ."

Judge Karl turned back to Alan. "Can it?"

"I'll lead you there myself!" Alan exclaimed, enthusiastically.

"Very well," Judge Karl ruled. "You shall remain in custody until the alleged barter is delivered to the State of Jefferson — receipt of which renders you free from obligation or debt."

Bang! The gavel slammed down. "Case closed," Judge Karl declared. "I'll be at the saloon."

~

Sean helped prepare the meal with Maia and twenty other hippie women, who chanted quietly as they worked.

Sean washed potatoes. "This home-cooked meal thing sure takes a lot of prep. You didn't have to do all this for me."

"We didn't," Maia explained. "We eat every meal from the ground up."

Sean tossed a peeled potato on the growing pile. "Well, that's great, if you have the time."

"Don't you?"

"Hell no," Sean replied. "McDonald's does breakfast all day long now. On my way home from work, I'll destroy two sausage McMuffin with eggs. Does the trick every time."

Maia was confused. "Do you eat at *the McDonald's* often?"

Shrugging, Sean replied, "I dunno, three, four times a week."

Maia seemed impressed. "They must be great friends."

Sean did a double take. "Wait. You've never heard of McDonald's?"

"No. They sound very generous. I'd like to meet them one day."

XVII

SCENE OF THE CRIME

The Scouts arrived with Cindy and took in the aftermath of what looked like a mighty struggle. The place was trashed – way more than what two drunk dudes could do.

Madison reviewed the carnage, stunned. "Oh, my God . . ."

Cindy turned her camera on, documenting as much as she could. "By the looks of all these spent shell casings . . ." She spun the camera around for a dramatic close-up. ". . . This wasn't just two guys shooting at beer bottles. Something went down. Something *bad*."

Oscar shouted from the other side of the camp, "Yo! Over here!" Cindy rushed to Oscar, who held up the tent, now shredded to pieces. "Looks grim, team."

"Guys, look!" Madison shouted. Oscar and Cindy joined her, pointing to the massive pile of bear crap. "Does a bear shit in the woods?"

"I guess so!" Oscar confirmed.

Madison spotted a rock, closer to where the guys ate dinner. She knelt down, noticing that the surface was smeared with a thick, red substance! "Dear God. Blood!"

"I thought so!" Cindy agreed. "This was a bear attack!"

"But where are the bodies?"

Oscar pointed his flashlight down the trail, away from the camp. "Hey! Two sets of prints! They may have survived – this way!"

~

Pit Bull unlocked Alan's jail cell and tossed an armful of clothes at him. "Ditch the hippie shit."

Alan looked at the clothing – all dark, synthetic and tactical – with dread. He looked up to Pit Bull and Ken Johnson, who sat casually on a desk. "Whoa. This is all military stuff."

"That's right," Ken Johnson confirmed. "We're going on a night op."

"Night . . . Op? Like . . . operation? *We?*"

"Get dressed!" Pit Bull barked.

Alan began to disrobe, nervously, as Ken Johnson explained. "You're the eyes and ears of Operation Barter Freedom."

"You gave it a name?"

"You know the location. You're 'First In.'"

"It's gotta be right now?"

Pit Bull stepped close to Alan, menacing. "Hurry up!"

Alan rolled his eyes and pulled on the tactical shirt. It was tight fitting and accentuated his Yoga-fit body.

Ken Johnson nodded. "The element of surprise is critical. Tactical strikes are always better under the cover of darkness."

Alan pulled on the tactical pants and cinched them tight. "I'm more of a late morning guy, but dude, let's be clear: I'm just gonna show you where the herb is. I'm not the one taking it."

Attorney General Maury stepped forward from the shadows and opened his book of rules. "Legally, according to Cascadian law, you would have to handle the 'barter' first, so that it came from you directly, not a third party."

Alan was befuddled. He grabbed the tactical boots and began to lace them up. "Man, for dudes who don't like a lot of rules – you sure got a lot of rules!"

~

An organic sound wailed throughout the grounds. A hippie crier stood on an upper balcony, blowing into a large conch shell. "Food, sisters! Gather! Gather!" she called out.

The hippies converged around an enormous, communal table, adorned liked it was Thanksgiving – albeit all organic. They remained standing, while Evenki gave the blessing. "We give thanks, Goddess of Love. Today, we celebrate the enduring power of the female. Power!"

The women joined in a loud chant of "Power! Power! Power!" Sean winced a little every time he heard the word.

The hippies sat and passed around plates bursting with every kind of fresh fruit and vegetable imaginable.

"So, the meat is coming out later?" Sean asked, casually. "I'm guessing it takes longer to cook."

Maia giggled. "It's not coming out at all, brother Heston. We're all vegans."

Sean looked at the food like it was suddenly strange.

A hippie walked around pouring wine from a chalice. "Strawberry wine?" she offered.

Sean shrugged, took a sip and was pleasantly surprised. "Great drinkability!" He turned to the wine hippie and stuck out his chalice. "Okay, fill 'er up!"

Sean smiled at Maia. She smiled back.

~

The compound was a buzz of last-minute battle prep. Cascadians hadn't seen this much action in a long time. Ken Johnson, bottle of cheap whiskey in hand, marched to the middle of the square with his team, Alan among them, now completely decked out like a cross between the Hells Angels and Desert Storm.

Ken Johnson gestured to the group at large. "Cascadia, circle up!"

The motley group gathered around a makeshift briefing area, complete with old map, nailed to a sheet of plywood.

Ken Johnson gestured to General Pierce, a craggy veteran, who stepped forward. "Men, a group of communist hippie women are squatting on State of Jefferson land. They are in possession of barter which is owed to the state. We have identified a greenhouse, containing a large marijuana 'grow-op.'"

The scruffy men, all drinking alcohol and smoking cigarettes, shook their heads in disgust.

"This is our target," the general continued. "The mission is to seize this contraband and return it to the State – by any means necessary." The general stepped away from the map to address his men directly. "Be warned, gentlemen, these hippie commies are godless. They have no morals. They'll use anything to defeat their enemies – narcotics, sorcery, satanism, hypnotism. Make as little eye contact as possible," he warned.

Alan raised a finger in protest. "Dude, these are hippies, not zombies."

But the general would have none of it. "*Trust* me. With this kind of adversary, being killed in battle is preferable to being captured."

The men took this in, solemnly. Ken Johnson raised his bottle for a toast. "Tonight, we fight for the State of Jefferson!"

Pit Bull seconded. "The State of Jefferson!"

To a hearty chorus of "State of Jefferson!" Ken Johnson took a swig from the plastic half liter and passed it around.

~

Sean was at the end of a long line of communal dishwashers. He dried and handed off to Maia, the grow-op queen. They had been spending most of the evening together.

"You're good at that, brother Sean. Do you do this at home?" Maia asked.

"Not at all. At home, Jenn does all the work," Sean replied.

"Jenn? Is that your wife?"

"No. Jenn-Air. Top of the line dishwasher."

Maia's face fell. "How sad."

The Crier blew her Conch again. "Gather, Sisters! To the Circle!"

Maia grabbed Sean's water-logged hands. "Quick, we have to get to the Relationship Seminar!"

"I'd rather wash dishes."

"Are you kidding?" Maia giggled. "You're the guest of honor!"

The hippie women all gathered around an elaborate, flower-covered ring in an open area. A small fire pit burned in the center.

Brigid and Eos stood inside the ring, holding hands. Brigid addressed the gathering. "Welcome, sisters. Tonight is a special night. We have been given a gift from the goddess of love. The gift of a stranger in need to give us perspective on our own relationships." Brigid gestured to Sean, whose head was already spinning. "The goddess of love wants you to share with us your thoughts on what makes a good relationship."

Sean lowered his head. "Boy, I dunno. That's, uh . . . that's awfully private."

"Secrets can be harmful to the soul," Brigid warned. "Be open. There is no judgement here."

Sean exhaled, defeatedly. Evenki the Shaman took Sean by the hand and entered the circle with him. She removed a handful of oddball stuff from her satchel and sprinkled it around, mumbling a prayer.

Brigid gestured to Sean's right hand. "I see a ring on your finger. Are you married?"

"That's what they say."

"How long?"

"Forever," Sean replied. Then, he calculated the time in his head. "Uh, twenty . . . *two* years, this August."

The hippies clapped appreciatively.

Brigid addressed the group. "We have a game called, 'When was the last time?' It is open to the women. Questions?"

The Hippies reacted excitedly. They loved this game. A number of hands shot up. Brigid chose random hippies.

"When was the last time you cleaned house?" the first hippie asked.

"The seventh of never," Sean replied.

"Do you have children?" the next hippie asked.

"I have a couple of monsters bleeding me dry, yeah. I'm still suspicious of the milk man, though."

"When was the last time you took your children to school?" came another question.

"Once. When the wife was sick. *Really* sick."

"When was the last time you helped with home-work?" another chimed in.

"My kids know the rules," Sean clarified. "They get the belt if they don't get a 3.3 GPA or higher."

"What was your GPA?" she asked.

"That's not the point," Sean deflected. "The idea is for each generation to be better than the one before. Sometimes, it takes a pat on the head. Sometimes, a little lower."

The Hippies didn't react well to threats of violence. Some women turned their backs to him.

"When was the last time you hugged your children?" a hippie asked.

"They know I love them," Sean replied.

"When was the last time you said you were sorry?" asked a woman.

Sean thought for a bit. Then a little more. "Been a while."

Maia offered up a question: "When was the last time you told your wife you loved her?"

Sean thought even longer. "I . . . don't remember."

A collective "Oooooooohhhhhhhh" emitted from the group.

"All right," Brigid said, calmly. "No judgment, but we think you can do better, brother Sean!"

"What's with the brother thing?" Sean countered. "I'm not related to any of you."

Maia raised her hand enthusiastically. "I propose that our visitor 'Walk a Mile.'"

"Great idea!" Brigid agreed.

"Yes!" shouted another random hippie.

Sean was really squirming. "I'm not sure if I like these games."

"Have you ever worn the clothes of a different gender?" Brigid asked.

"Well, sure. Once. In college. But I was *really* drunk."

"In order to appreciate your wife – and the sacrifices she has made – it's time to walk as a woman."

"No. I'm good. I have enough trouble walking as a middle-aged man," Sean elaborated.

"To see the other side, this is what you need," Brigid encouraged.

"No, what I need is a hot bath and two fingers of bourbon."

A group of hippie women began to converge around Sean, led by Bast, the militant one. "Ok, c'mon," he pleaded. "I get the idea. I can use my imagination, you know . . . we don't have to . . ."

All at once, a dozen chanting women laid their hands on Sean. Ritualistically, they spun him in a loose circle, simultaneously removing articles of his clothing.

What was that powder being poured in Sean's mouth?

His vision blurred. His speech slowed. He was becoming lost in space.

~

Each Cascadian had a turn taking a swig until the two-thirds empty bottle got to Alan. He looked to Ken Johnson, who looked back, expectantly.

Alan, no longer a stranger to alcohol, drained the rest of the harsh liquid, tossed the plastic bottle into the dirt and wiped his lips with his sleeve like an old-time desperado. The men around him cheered.

Ken Johnson pulled out a semi-automatic pistol from his belt and tossed it to Alan. "Cascadians are Second Amendment lovers. You?"

Alan skillfully took off the safety and proceeded to blast away at the empty whiskey bottle, spinning it around the square until finally shredding it into a million pieces – much to the merriment of the Cascadians, including Ken Johnson.

"Welcome to the fold, Cascadian!" Ken Johnson congratulated Alan. He turned to his men. "Let's go get that shit!!!"

The Cascadians, itching for action, marched off and mounted up.

Alan lamented his plastic litter. "That's gonna wind up in the ocean. Bummer."

~

Cindy walked behind the Scouts as they hustled through the night, scanning with their Scout-issued flashlights for fresh tracks in the sand. "Let's face it, these guys could be horribly mauled beyond recognition."

"I don't see any drag marks," Madison replied. "They could be perfectly fine, Cindy. You media types are so over the top."

"I'm just being realistic. We have to be ready to see images that will haunt our dreams."

Oscar had had enough of this. "Hey, stay focused on the task at hand, alright? We're looking for signs of life, not death."

Then – in the distance – a soft, lilting musical sound. Madison shushed the group and they stopped to listen. "What is that?"

Oscar listened intently. "Sounds musical."

Cindy looked around in thought. "Sounds like a lute."

Oscar held a finger over his mouth to silence them. He pointed toward the sound, indicating for them to follow as he headed off.

~

The Hippie transformation chant was intensifying as more women swirled around Sean. Articles of women's clothing were being brought in and out of the increasing circle of celebrants.

The chant rose to a primal wail, not unlike a Xena episode. Evenki's arms went wide, calling out, "Sean-dra . . . EMERGE!"

The women parted and "Sean-dra" emerged all right – he was a full-blown, hippie Priscilla of the Desert! This macho man was now adorned with make-up, scarves, jewelry and flow-y, semi-revealing clothing. The image was captivating, if nothing else.

The hippie women surrounding him cheered and clapped in approval and acceptance.

"You are beautiful!" Brigid confirmed.

Sean was too far gone to back out now. Tears welled in his eyes as he scanned the mind-blowing crowd of new-agers. "I am, aren't I?"

From a ridge at the edge of the Hippie compound, Cindy and the Scouts found the source of the hypnotic music – a sophisticated hippie enclave in the middle of a borderline-frightening, primal celebration.

Oscar noticed that one particular hippie wasn't quite as "delicate" as the others. He tapped Cindy on the shoulder and pointed. "Check that out. Zoom in."

Cindy was already in the process and the trio huddled around her small monitor as it isolated the lumbering, out-of-step hippie.

Oscar squinted at the small screen. "Holy shit – is that . . . ?"

Madison shoved Oscar out of the way and looked closer. Her face blanched. ". . . Mr. Heston?"

Sean unconsciously rubbed his hands across his body in exploration, then spun, sending a colorful array of fabric swirling in the air around him. Total hippie overload.

Cindy addressed her camera. "It appears, as plain as the fringe on his dress, incumbent conservative candidate Sean Heston has joined a feral, hippie cult of women! This might be the political 180 of the YEAR!"

But before her report was finished, Cindy was interrupted by the sound of loud, poorly maintained vehicles approaching. Cindy and the Scouts turned their attention to the intruders – the Cascadians – approaching in full bad-ass mode!

Oscar tapped Cindy on the shoulder, pointing like mad. "Over there!"

Cindy brushed his hand away and barked, "I'm zooming, I'm zooming!" Her camera settled on Ken Johnson, bouncing along in the side car of the motorcycle, driven by Pit Bull, then panned to spot Alan, riding atop the running boards of a stake-bed style truck, driven by General Pierce. Alan was dressed to the nines, drinking whiskey out of a flask, AR-15 thrust in the air excitedly.

Cindy gulped at the image. "Oh, boy . . ."

The rest of the Cascadians followed in self-repaired/modified motorcycles or 4-wheel drive vehicles – even an old ambulance. Mad Max without a budget.

Cindy spun the camera back on herself. "In a startling development, it appears that Alan Rosenbaum, incredibly liberal opposition candidate has joined a radical, right-wing anti-government group! He is armed to the teeth and appears to be consuming an alcoholic beverage from an open container! Talk about a political 180! This might be a 270!," she exclaimed, as she swung the camera back toward the action.

The Ecotopia Hippie Crier spotted the armada approaching and blew her primal alarm, albeit way too late! The sound from her Conch was drowned out by the lack of mufflers on the invading vehicles and flash bang grenades, tossed by Cascadians to distract and confuse.

CRASH! The stake bed truck rammed the gate, sending celebrating hippie women scattering everywhere.

Cindy and the Scouts were getting great footage as they moved about the compound in stealth mode, trying not to be seen.

The diesel spewing vehicles circled in the main square as Alan eyeballed the greenhouse.

Pointing, Alan shouted, "There's the barter!"

General Pierce nodded tightly. "Right!" The stake bed truck turned sharply, sending another group of hippies, including Sean, running for safety.

As Sean turned back to look at the invaders, time slowed as he made eye contact with Alan. Both men were completely out of their element – stoned, drunk, dressed really differently – not even sure how they got where they were now.

In ultra-slow-motion, Alan's eyes bulged in disbelief. "YOU?!"

Even slower, Sean reacted, incredulous. "YOU?!"

Seeing each other snapped them out of their reverie and time returned to normal. As Alan raced past, he raised the butt of his rifle and – WHACK – laid Sean out cold.

The truck lumbered toward the greenhouse, signaling distress among the defenders.

Maia, queen of the grow-op, was aghast. "Protect the greenhouse!" she bellowed.

Too late – Alan and his stake bed buddies careened into the greenhouse as Cascadians descended from every angle. Alan grabbed pot plants two at a time and hurled them up to several guys on the truck.

As well as pot theft, the Cascadians were engaged in an overall campaign of terror – grappling hooks and ropes knocked down stalls, gazebos and fencing, while windows were smashed and fires were set, Molotov cocktail style. Ken Johnson gleefully barked orders all the way.

As he loaded pot plants, Alan reacted to the sounds of chaos outside and turned to Ken Johnson. "Dude, what's going on out there? We're just here to pick up my pot, not start World War III!"

"The godless commies are squatting on State of Jefferson land," Ken Johnson clarified. "They have to pay the price." He turned to Pit Bull. "Take it all!"

Alan objected. "Whoa. We said half. Not all. You can't change the deal!"

Ken looked to Attorney General Maury, who pointed to a passage. "Eminent Domain. It's right here."

Alan sized up Ken Johnson. "I see. Ok. Man, I guess you're just a low-quality individual."

"With *high quality* weed. Go back to your tribe, interloper!" Whack! Ken Johnson knocked Alan cold with the butt of his gun and headed toward his sidecar. "Move out!!!"

The stake bed rolled out the other side of the greenhouse, overloaded with pot plants, taking tubing, bags of fertilizer and sundry grow-op elements with it. The truck made a full circle, exiting the compound the way it came in.

The Cascadian Convoy of Doom regrouped outside the compound and rolled away into the desert darkness, leaving the ranch in smoldering ruins.

Hiding off in the bushes, Cindy lowered her camera. Tears streamed down her face.

Oscar, completely agape, tapped her on the shoulder. "Did you get it?"

Cindy nodded and wiped a tear. "All of it."

~

As day broke in the Oregon desert, the aftermath of the attack was visible. Tears fell. Wounds were tended. Hippies did their best to clean up, but the place was now basically uninhabitable.

Brigid made the rounds with her wife, Eos, consoling their sisters. Brigid came upon Sean sitting off to one side, rubbing his sore temple, generally feeling like shit.

Alan limped out of the wrecked greenhouse, taking in the desolation. Dressed like a biker/rebel, he was quite the visual anomaly. "Whoa. This is so. Fucked. Up."

Brigit spotted Alan and walked up. Pissed. "Wow, Alan. Really? On this day of all days, you couldn't just let it go?"

Alan tried to calm her down. "Oh, no, honestly, Brigid – this is just a random coincidence . . ."

"I finally find someone I can truly love, someone who knows how to LOVE ME BACK. You could have been happy for me, but no – you had to ruin it!"

WHACK! Brigid laid Alan out with a solid right, sending him sprawling to the dust.

Sean looked down at Alan. "You two know each other?"

Alan rubbed his jaw. "We used to be married."

Sean turned away, stifling a laugh.

Brigid turned her attention toward Sean and Alan. "You two have brought violence and greed to this land. Everything we are against. You must go and never return."

Sean stood up, slowly, painfully. "No."

Brigid was taken aback. "Excuse me?"

"This isn't right. Those guys say you're trespassing. You have the deed to this property?"

Brigid nodded. "Locked up in the safe."

"And your grow-op is legal, right?"

"It is. We have the paperwork. What's your point?"

"You haven't done anything illegal," Sean explained. "Those assholes are full of shit. *They* are the squatters. *They* stole your legal weed. Even here, in the middle of the Oregon wilderness, the rule of law still applies." Sean kicked at the dirt, repentant. "Now, look, my 'associate' and I, we fucked you over. No question about it. This is our bad. We want to make this right."

Brigid was unconvinced. "How?"

Sean gestured to Alan. "We're gonna go and get your pot back."

Alan did a double take. "We are?"

"Yep. I don't know how, but we'll figure something out, right, Alan?"

Covering, Alan responded. "Uh . . . yeah. Of course."

Brigid stepped forward. "You'll need our help."

Sean smirked. "That's nice, but all you have are weapons that Fred Flintstone would use."

Bast loaded a rock into her sling, whipped it around and let it go. The sharp projectile ricocheted off a tree, then off a stone wall, then into Sean's forehead, dropping him to his knees.

Sean shook his head to make his eyes uncross. "Ok. That's cool, but you may have to actually physically fight these guys. You ready for that?"

Bast signaled to Eos, Brigid's timid wife. She raced up to Alan and flipped him on his head in two seconds, Ju Jitsu style.

Alan reacted, rubbing his sore butt. "Whoa."

Sean wobbled back to his feet. "I take it back. Maybe you *can* help. You know anything about where they are?"

"Dude! Yeah. I was there. I saw it!" Alan announced. "It was a freakin' ghost town . . . called Cramp, or something."

Brigid's eye lit up in recognition. "Crump. The old mining town. It's our family name. It's on the property. We have the plans in the safe."

Sean suddenly forgot about his forehead. "Then let's get busy. We'll hit 'em tonight."

Sean and Brigid nodded in solidarity. Brigid nodded to Bast, who nodded to her warriors — they know what to do.

~

At dusk, battle preparations began:

Stink bombs were assembled . . .

Rocks/slings were gathered, loaded . . .

Blow darts were tied, tested . . .

Potatoes were bagged . . .

Ropes were coiled . . .

Hippies changed from "day wear" to "night mode," with the same flow-y feel, but now in muted colors for darkness.

Sean and Alan each changed into their own version of badass hippie warriors.

The ancient blueprint for the mining town of Crump was rolled out on a charred table.

Brigid pointed out the best hits. "We can access an abandoned mine shaft outside of town, here. The shaft leads right to the edge of Crump, over here."

Sean approved. "Perfect. They'll never see us coming."

Bast addressed Sean. "We locate the pot. Disable the guards. Commandeer the truck. Get our stuff back."

Cindy, Madison and Oscar, still on site, had been watching intently. Cindy found the right moment to approach Brigid. "Excuse, me, Miss Brigid? I want to enlist in the fight."

"Oh, sweetie, that's so nice, but this isn't your fight. It could be dangerous. And you're too young."

"I'm sixteen and emancipated."

Brigid smiled warmly. "Aren't we all, sister. Okay, if you're willing to take the risk and actually help, we would love to have you."

Cindy practically jumped up and down. "Oh my God, thank you! I'll make you proud!"

"You already have." Brigid called out, "Ladies get her dressed!"

The hippies whisked Cindy away. Brigid turned to Madison and Oscar. "And you two?"

Oscar and Madison exchanged a nervous glance.

"Oh, I'm good. I'm not emancipated," Madison explained. "I'm way past my curfew already."

Oscar gestured to Sean and Alan. "Yeah, besides, we have Scouts orders. We have to report back on these candidates."

Brigid looked at Sean and Alan. "Candidates? These two?"

The candidates nodded, proudly.

Brigid laughed out loud. "Well thanks for that. Best laugh I've had all day! Ecotopians, let's do this!"

The hippies, armed primitively, moved out under the cover of darkness, disappearing into the desert countryside.

Oscar and Madison watched them go. Oscar fumbled for his walkie-talkie and keyed the microphone. "Scout Recon to base, do you read me?"

After a moment, a crackling voice transmitted. "We copy, Scout Recon. What is your Sit Rep?"

Oscar didn't even know where to start but advised, "You better get the sheriff to the old mining town of Crump ASAP, because the Ecotopians are about to attack the Cascadians!"

There was a moment of dead air on the radio, then, ". . . The who are doin' what? Where?"

~

It was time to celebrate a major Cascadian victory. The guys circled around a bonfire in the central square, passing whiskey around while Ken Johnson gave a rallying speech. "Fellow Cascadians, tonight, we celebrate a great victory. This wasn't just about liberating contraband, this was about freedom, unity and the State of Jefferson!"

The men clapped appreciatively.

From the mine shaft, just beyond earshot, a group of dark warriors emerged from the shadows. Sean, Alan, Brigid and Bast led the way. They scoped out the surroundings.

Across the town, outside the old livery stable, multiple armed guards patrolled lazily.

Sean singled them out. "There's your dope. Those guards tell the whole story."

Bast reiterated the plan. "We'll go in three teams. Prevent. Disable. Attain."

Sean looked at Bast, a little surprised. "You don't talk much like a hippie."

"I was a hippie. Then I was a soldier. Iraq. Afghanistan. Now, I'm a hippie again," Bast explained.

Sean smiled, appreciatively, offering his hand. "Appreciate your service. I'm a Desert Storm vet myself. What branch?"

"Marines."

Again, Sean was surprised. "What assignment?"

"Special Ops. You?"

"Uh . . . re-supply."

Bast smiled appreciatively. "Appreciate your service." She then signaled and the first team moved out.

As they slid through the darkness, the first team put sand in gas tanks, emptied the air out of tires and put potatoes in mufflers – all the low-tech ways to disable vehicles.

In the square, Ken Johnson continued. ". . . We are accused of many things. To the old ways of thinking, we are thieves, squatters, merchants of violence and intimidation. But do we represent the old ways?"

The group responded with a resounding, "Hell no!"

"No! We are *new freedom*. New freedom isn't based on some smelly old documents. New freedom is immediate! You see it, you take it! Freedom isn't free unless it's totally free!"

The men cheered again. And drank more.

The second team of warriors spotted four perimeter guards. They inched close enough to launch sedated blow darts. Each guard reacted like getting an insect bite, but within seconds, they got woozy and collapsed.

Ken Johnson wasn't done bullshitting. ". . . New Freedom is so new it still has an umbilical cord! We must cherish and nurture the little Baby Freedom . . ."

Bast coordinated with an archer who wrapped a stink bomb around an arrow and launched it high into the air. The arrow landed dead center in the middle of the fire and began to emit a dingy smoke.

". . . Oh, Sure, Baby Freedom is going to have some growing pains," Ken Johnson' continued. "Baby Freedom, at some point, will shit the bed . . ."

The men didn't understand, but it didn't matter. They clapped anyway.

Another hippie with a slingshot launched a glass vile directly into a large pot of chili that guys were making as part of their celebration. A dark red liquid seeped into the gruel. Oblivious, hungry dudes lined up, anxious for a cup.

Ken Johnson's speech went on still. "In its adolescence, Teenager New Freedom is going to have pimples and ejaculate prematurely, but we can't let awkward interludes get in the way of caring for our child. Ugly, or beautiful, Baby New Freedom is ours to love!"

"Hooray!" the Cascadians cheered.

With the perimeter softened, the final team moved up to the livery stable. Sean and Alan were part of this group, as well as Cindy, now looking ninja bad ass, with a GoPro strapped to the side of her head.

On cue, hippie warriors swung their slings and launched sharp rocks – severely aggravating and distracting the guards. Immediately following the rocks, ninja warriors moved in to dispatch them.

The remaining hippies scaled the livery stable walls and dropped stink bombs down several air vents from the roof.

Inside, the stink bombs erupted in a purple haze. Two guards looked at each other stupidly. One guard tried to speak, "Hey, what the fuuu–" but he didn't finish his sentence.

Another guard tried to sound the alarm, but he, too, was overwhelmed by the fumes.

Two Ninja women with face masks zip lined from an upper window and removed the beam blocking the large stable doors. The women kicked it in unison and the doors opened wide with a rusty groan.

Sean and Allen raced inside, leapt into the truck and fired it up. Sean turned to Alan. "Ain't no going back now. You ready for this . . . partner?"

Alan flashed a dopey thumbs up. "As ready as I'll ever be . . . partner. Let's ride!"

Sean put the stake bed into gear. It lurched out of the delivery stable and into the main compound. Drunk Cascadian's reacted, albeit slowly. To their disbelief, they saw Allen and Sean driving directly toward the exit!

Pit Bull spotted the invaders. "Breach!!"

The men collectively fumbled, ass over tea kettle, to get their bearings, let alone weapons. As each Cascadian attempted to hop on a ride, get a gun, run after the truck, whatever, they were each foiled:

- Bonk! A rock knocked a dude off his Harley.

- Clump! A guy's spiked chili fell out of his hand, followed by him falling face down in the dirt.

- Flap, flap, flap! – Flat tires crippled vehicles large and small.

- Trip. Thump. Bump – the Cascadians fell one by one.

- Fud-dud-dud – Ken Johnson's sidecar wouldn't start, via the old potato in the tail pipe gag, leaving him furious. "What the hell is going –?" But he couldn't finish, because he was now unconscious.

In the stake bed, Sean and Alan were having a great time.

"I must say, in all my years, I never thought I'd be doing anything like this," Sean admitted. "I dunno about you, but I am *way* out of my comfort zone."

Alan agreed. "About as far as I can get, brother. Not that I'm complaining!"

Then, across the windshield, a bright light swept back-and-forth and a wind from overhead kicked up gravel and sand. Sean and Allen looked up to see a Sheriff Department helicopter hovering directly above.

Alan looked to Sean. "Whoa. What did they used to say in the old gangster movies, brother?"

"The jig is up?"

"That's the one."

Sheriff Ziegler, a "former" athlete, surveyed the area from his high vantage point. There was very little activity. It seemed like everyone was dead. The sheriff keyed the microphone on his loudspeaker and focused on the rolling stake bed. "Attention! This is the Dryer County Sheriff's department. You are under arrest! Exit the vehicle and throw down your weapons!" He turned to his pilot and remarked, "Good lord above. I thought hippies were peace lovers. They just massacred an entire town!"

HOUSE DIVIDED

XVIII

RECKONING

A light breeze blew outside the Dryer County Courthouse. A slightly frayed American flag flapped incessantly.

Inside, locals shuffled into the packed courthouse. This could be the hearing of the century – at least in Dryer, Oregon. Alan, Sean, the hippies, the Cascadians were all present, looking sunburned and a little worse for wear.

The Bailiff addressed the court. "All rise for the honorable Dobb Dryer!"

Yes, Dobb Dryer was also the judge. It was a small town. Dobb took his seat and centered himself atop his O-ring inflatable cushion. "Be seated!" Dobb reviewed a stack of paperwork in front of him. "Let me see if I got this straight: Incumbent candidate Sean Heston sought refuge with an all-female commune of squatters, while opposing candidate . . ." He squinted at the paperwork and continued, "Alan . . ."

"Rosembaum . . ." Alan reminded him.

". . . Teamed up with the separatist organization State of Jefferson to steal pot from these same hippies. Is that about right?"

Brigid, the representative for the hippies, stood, holding a stack of ancient documents. "Excuse me, your honor, you're talking about my property. We're not squatters. I have the deed right here."

"Uh-huh. And who are you?" Dobb asked.

"I am Brigid, your honor. Owner of the property. I founded Ecotopia. I am a triple goddess – maiden, mother, wise."

Dobb looked up from his paperwork, letting that hang for a moment. "Uh-huh. What about this pot?"

Brigid passed a document up to Dobb. "It is a legal grow, your honor. I have the registration number."

Dodd reviewed the paperwork. "Uh-huh. And Mr. Rosen-bam, did you join this State of Jefferson?"

Alan held up his right hand like he was taking an oath. "Nay your honor. In fact, those dudes arrested me."

"For what?"

"Trespassing."

"Uh-huh," Dobb responded, scanning the courtroom. "Okay, so this State of Jefferson. Who runs the show?"

Maury, the Attorney General was quick to rise. "Your honor, I am the counsel for the State of Jefferson."

A glint of recognition registered with Dobb. "Yes, Maury Podnik, I know all about you. You were disbarred about five years ago, isn't that correct?"

Maury attempted to object. "Your honor, the State of Oregon has no jurisdiction over the State of Jefferson, whom I represent."

"You can't represent *your mother* in this courtroom, sir," Dobb snapped. "You will sit down and shut your mouth, or I'll have you thrown in jail – a *real* one!"

Ken Johnson cleared his throat and stood. "Uh, your honor. I'm Ken Johnson, Governor of the State of Jefferson."

Dobb leaned back in his overstuffed, leather chair. "Very well, 'Governor' Ken Johnson. Why were you trying to steal their legal weed?"

"Well, sir, we were receiving recompense for damages inflicted on our mining operation."

Dodd perked up at this revelation. "Oh? Got the permit on file with the minerals office, do you?"

Ken Johnson and Maury looked at each other. Gulp.

"No? There's a shocker." Dobb fixed his gaze on Sean. "Okay, so, Sean, uh, Mr. Heston. Please stand."

Sean rose hesitantly.

"It's no secret. We've known each other a long time. Since when do you hang out with hippies?" Dobb asked.

Sean flexed his trick knee. "I was rehabbing a hiking injury, sir."

"And you became so enamored with their cause, you helped them steal marijuana?"

"Steal it *back*, your honor. These idiots from Crump stole it first."

Dobb turned back to Brigid. "Uh-huh. Now, Miss Hippie Queen, did the 'so-called' State of Jefferson inflict damages to your compound?"

Brigid passed some pictures up to Dobb for inspection. "Yes, your honor, it's . . . destroyed."

Dobb looked at the pictures and shook his head. "Funny, in this digital age, there's no video to back up anybody's story. And we even had a real news reporter on the job," Dobb said, looking at his papers. "Cindy Chan, where are you?"

Cindy, now with a little hippie flair to her dress, stood. "Here, your honor."

"You're a camera-person, are you?" Dobb asked.

"Yes, sir. Intern. KDRY."

"Well, that's great. Okay, so, you'll forgive me if I'm a little confused why you don't have any footage of this?"

Cindy was on the spot. She looked to Sean, who looked to Alan, who looked to Ken Johnson, who looked to Maury, who shrugged.

"It's . . . the Oregon desert, sir," Cindy explained. "Known for *harsh* conditions. My storage chips suffered from . . . Digital *Refraction* . . . due to . . . the elements."

Dobb wrinkled his nose. "Is that an actual term?"

". . . Yes, your honor."

Dobb leaned back and clucked to himself. "Okay, here's the deal: The State of Jefferson is not a state, so you can stop all that sovereign horse pucky. The term for you is 'squatters' — and as such, you have forty-eight hours to vacate the premises of Crump. As punishment, you, Ken Johnson and your affiliates will provide sweat equity toward the repair of Ecotopia, otherwise known as The Cripple Creek Ranch. Additionally, you and your State of Jefferson affiliates shall wear sandwich board style placards which read, 'I am an ignorant jerk,' twenty-four hours a day for thirty days."

Bang! Dobb slammed his gavel down hard, startling the packed room. "Case closed!" Dobb looked at his watch. "Will you look at that. It's Happy Hour. What the hell are we doing here? See you at Shemp's!"

The exonerated group broke into a spontaneous cheer and the gallery followed suit.

HOUSE DIVIDED

XIX

HOMECOMING

Doris, Ronald and Nancy entered the family home, followed by a very humbled Sean, holding his "release from jail" bag of women's clothing.

Doris closed the door firmly. "Family meeting." She indicated for Sean to sit on the living room couch while the other three stood in front of him. "Okay. Let's have it," Doris demanded. "An apology. An explanation. *Something.*"

Sean cleared his throat. "Um. I'm sorry that I . . . got some bad advice from my staff . . ."

Doris wasn't buying it. "A *real* apology. You screwed up, Buster Brown. Take some goddamn responsibility."

Little Ronald was aghast. "Mom! Language!"

Doris snapped a finger in his little face. "Quiet!"

Sean put his hands up. "Okay. Okay. This was 100% my fault. I was a jerk. I was weak. Things . . . got out of hand. You don't have to accept it, but I apologize. To all of you. I never meant for any of this to happen."

Doris calmed down a bit. "You do know how painfully small this town is, don't you?"

Sean nodded, embarrassed. "Yes, I do. *Painfully*."

Doris took the bag from Sean and poked through it, examining the outfit. "Please tell me that wearing women's clothing at an all-women hippie retreat while tripping on hallucinogens was purely for tactical purposes."

Sean hesitated. "It was . . . a long story – which I'm a little uncomfortable talking about in front of the children."

Nancy had enough of her idiot father. "It's too late, dad! Everyone already knows you were tripping with commie lesbians!"

Sean stood in defense, addressing the group. "Now, you are aware that I have a trick knee, right? This all started because of a simple painkiller."

Nancy's laugh was full of scorn. "Diaeme is not a simple painkiller, dad. We Googled it!"

Doris folded her arms. "How did it feel?"

"The Diaeme?"

"The women's clothing,"

"Is that a loaded question?" Sean asked.

"No."

"It was really comfortable. Minus the G-string," Sean confessed.

Little Ronald covered his ears. "Dad! Gross!"

Not letting it go, Nancy pressed. "How was the Diaeme?"

Sean looked at Doris, with pleading eyes. "Do I have to answer that?"

"You might as well," Doris reasoned.

Sean hesitated, then looked right at Nancy. "It was . . . *horrible! Don't do drugs!*"

Nancy rolled her eyes. "Nice try."

Doris changed her tact. "You spent two days in what some men would consider nirvana. You didn't learn anything about female empowerment?"

"Of course I did," Sean replied.

"What?"

Sean looked at the floor. "Not to mess with it."

Doris kissed Sean on the forehead and removed the bag of clothing. "You need a shower, honey. You reek."

After her mom was gone, Nancy added, "Like pot."

Sean made eye contact with his daughter. "Well, that would make sense, wouldn't it, smarty pants? I was surrounded by hippies."

Nancy was intrigued. "Okay, so, dad. Did you inhale?"

Sean considered before speaking. "I am older than twenty-one. Marijuana is legal, medically – and recreationally – in the state of Oregon. Draw your own conclusions." With that, Sean slouched into his bedroom and shut the door.

Little Ronald turned to his sister. "If it's any consolation, he seems like less of a dick now."

~

Alan was back home to his mother Esther and his cats and his plants.

"So, the great anarchist has returned," Esther said, dryly. "Lucky for you it wasn't in a body bag."

"Wonderful to see you too, mom," Alan replied. "You didn't say hello at the hearing."

"And let people know we're related? Not a chance."

Alan dumped a dusty leather bag on the floor and started to peel off layers of grungy clothing.

"So. You lost," Esther said, reviewing a copy of the *Dryer Bugle*.

"We both did. But we won."

Esther waved the paper in the air. "How do you figure? Even your own parties dumped you!"

Alan turned to his mother, pointedly. "We're two opposites who figured out a way to tolerate each other."

"Why bother trying to work with an ideological creep?"

"He's a solid guy, mom. We're not, like, fishing dudes or anything, but he's not as bogus as he seems."

Alan peeled off a layer of camouflaged long under-wear and tossed it on his bed in the next room.

"And what's with the militant look?" his mother asked, concerned. "Did you take over a Wildlife Refuge?"

Alan would normally suffer the abuse his mother doled out, but he was no longer intimidated. "Hey, mom, you know the one thing I learned in the desert? How to stand up for myself. So, guess what? From now on, I'm not gonna let you talk to me like that."

"Like what?"

"Down to me. Like I'm an idiot."

"You are an idiot."

Alan stepped close, to face Esther. "No I'm not, mom. I *never* was. So, you're not gonna talk *down* to me and I'm not gonna talk *up* to you. We're either going to talk to each other like adults, or we're not going talk to each other at all."

Esther was fairly astonished at the new behavior of her son, but she wasn't going to push it. "Well . . . since you feel so strongly about it . . ."

"Yes, mother. That's the word. *Strong*. I'm feeling *strong!*" Alan declared.

"You're different. What happened to you in the desert?"

"Everything. Now, I'm gonna take a nice warm shower and go to the bar."

Esther blanched. "Since when do you drink?"

"You know what's awesome? I don't have to answer that," and Alan slammed the door to his room.

"When will you be home?" Esther prodded.

"Or *that!*" Alan shouted from behind the door.

~

Shemp's Trading Post was a county institution for no real good reason, other than the fact that it was once a stage stop along the Oregon Trail. On this night, pretty much everyone in Dryer was there. It was a lively place, packed with Western historical knickknacks.

Sean entered, leading Doris by the hand. He was nervous and embarrassed, trying to be low key, but locals spotted him right away and shared a mixed vocal reaction – anything from "Atta boy, Sean!" to "Commie lover!"

Already perched at the bar were Dobb, Ken Johnson, newlyweds Brigid & Eos – all having beers and shots. Sean and Doris joined the eclectic group as Pauly, the crusty bartender tossed a few napkins on the table.

"Doris? Same?" Pauly asked.

"Yes. Thanks, Pauly," she replied.

"Sean?"

Sean hesitated. "I'll just have an iced tea."

Pauly raised an eyebrow. "Oh? Are we under the weather? Financial crisis? Mars in retrograde?"

"Just an iced tea, Pauly."

"I don't know you," Pauly replied, looking at Sean like he was crazy.

Alan arrived. He got the same array of cat calls, ranging from "That hippie could hunt!" to "Pot thief!"

Sean was happy to see his new friend and turned back to the bartender. "Pauly, my fellow desert adventurer is parched from his travels. Alan? Aloe vera juice? Agave nectar?"

Alan smiled, but shook his head no. "Bourbon. Double. Neat."

"At least *someone* around here knows how to drink," Pauly smirked. "Comin' right up."

Alan looked to Sean and winked. Sean revealed a vape pen in his pocket and winked back. "I don't know about you, but in a way, this is all a big relief."

"Not going to jail? No doubt," Alan agreed. "Incarceration is creepy and draconian."

"No, I mean we're free. No more money to raise . . . No more hands to shake . . ."

"No more fossils fuels to burn," Alan added.

Doris chimed in with, "No more hair appointments, no more boring speeches . . ."

"Mean debates . . ."

"Party platforms . . ."

"Asses to kiss!"

Pauly delivered the first round of drinks.

Sean grabbed his tea and announced, "A toast! To getting kicked out of our own parties! To freedom!"

The three clinked and drank.

"It is appealing," Sean continued, looking at Doris. "No party. No pandering." He turned to Alan and continued, "We could each run as *independents*."

"Separately? All over again?" Alan asked.

"That's how it works. Voters want a choice – one or the other."

"Brother Sean, the Yin and the Yang are opposite shapes," Alan offered. "But together they make the whole. Nobody wants to be a Yinless Yang, or a Yangless Yin."

"What are you getting at?" Sean asked, intrigued.

Doris reached for her drink. "Don't include me in this folly."

"If we run together," Alan continued, "people can get a little of this and a little of that – they wouldn't have to vote for the full monty in any one direction."

"But you're forcing their hand," Sean argued. "Voters couldn't have one without the other."

Alan sipped from his bourbon and shrugged. "Aren't the best solutions the ones that piss everyone off – just a little bit?"

"You feel like pissing everyone off?"

"I kinda do," Alan admitted. "Just a little bit."

"Then we should do it!"

The boys clinked their bourbon and iced tea glasses to seal the deal.

Doris was mortified. "Jesus H. Christ. Here we go again," she grumbled, holding up her empty glass. "Pauly!!"

HOUSE DIVIDED

XX

NOT YOUR FATHER'S CAMPAIGN

Everyone was participating somehow in the new, unorthodox campaign.

The hippie bus was in full gear, stopping often, flooding main street with colorful hippie women, handing out hemp campaign leaflets . . .

The Scouts were mobilized, led by Oscar and Madison. They gave joint speeches about conflict – and ways to resolve them – in schools, malls, libraries . . .

Cascadians were pitching in as well, offering security services and essentially being the motorcade for the united candidates as they made their way across Dryer County . . .

Sean and Alan went door to door, sharing ideas with locals, still contradicting each other at every step . . .

Out with a group of hunters, Sean tried to seal the deal. "Good news, fellas – this administration loves guns!"

"Just not for everyone!" Alan chimed in.

Talking to a shirtless guy, Alan shared a plank from their platform. "We're *soft* on childcare!"

And Sean added, "But, we're *strong* on military!"

Lighting up with a stoner, Alan shared their plan. "We'll preserve the environment!"

Sean grabbed the joint and took a long hit. ". . . But not at the expense of business!"

The campaign was just weird enough to work. With virtually no opposition, our boys were ushered into office.

The *Dryer Bugle* headline said it all, declaring:

CONFLICT NO MORE!
JOINT TICKET WINS IN LANDSLIDE VICTORY!
EVERYONE IS PISSED – JUST A LITTLE BIT!

~

Outside the Dryer County Administration offices, Sean's Humvee and Alan's Prius pulled up and parked in freshly painted Commissioner spots, side by side. The gents got out, nodded to each other and walked together toward the utilitarian building.

Cindy Chan, back on the job, met them with camera in hand. "So, commissioners. Defeated as adversaries. Victorious as allies. Your takeaway from the stunning victory?"

Sean couldn't fully shake the way he spoke as a career politician. He smiled broadly, with "I think you summed it up perfectly, Cindy."

Alan butted in. "And I hear congrats is in order too!"

Cindy blushed. "Yeah, thanks! Because the story went viral, I got an offer to do field work in the Medford market."

Sean patted Cindy on the shoulder. "Wow, that's great, Cindy. Next stop, Sacramento!"

"Maybe. Okay, one final question, before I let you get down to the business of county government: being that you still have major political differences, how will you decide which decision 'wins?'"

Alan and Sean looked at each other and chuckled. "That's easy," they explained, in tandem, "Rock, paper, scissors!"

Sean and Alan bid their pleasant goodbyes and entered the building, toward their respective offices – Sean's on the right, Alan's on the left.

THE END

Cover, Illustrations & Design
by
Craig "Kif" Sanborn

Made in the USA
Las Vegas, NV
13 January 2024

84263215R00085